CANDY CANE DREAMS

Mistletoe Meadows
Book 6

JESSIE GUSSMAN

Contents

Acknowledgments

Cover art by Covers and Cupcakes
Editing by Heather Hayden
Narration by Jay Dyess
Author Services by CE Author Assistant

Listen to the unabridged audio for FREE performed by Jay Dyess on the Say with Jay channel on YouTube. Get early access to all of Jay's recordings and listen to Jessie's books before they're available to the general public, plus get daily Bible readings by Jay and bonus scenes by becoming a Say with Jay channel member.

Books in the Mistletoe Meadows Sweet Christmas romance series:
1. Sleigh Bell Dreams
2. Icicle Dreams
3. Sugarplum Dreams
4. Christmas Dreams
5. Holly Jolly Dreams
6. Candy Cane Dreams
7. Mistletoe Dreams

Chapter One

Kate Woolbert tightened her grip on the steering wheel and watched the snowflakes as they fell lazily down, drifting up and over her car windshield as she drove through the sleepy town of Mistletoe Meadows.

The street lights, with large lighted outlines of Christmas trees, candy canes, or snowmen anchored around them, made the snow glisten and glitter as it slid past her car as she motored slowly down the street.

Everything she owned was in her car, although she wasn't thinking about that as she looked at the dark storefront windows that somehow, despite the early hour and the lack of anyone walking around, still managed to seem warm and welcoming.

She left Baltimore shortly after midnight because she hadn't been able to sleep. She still had several hours before she was supposed to meet with Principal Stevens about her new job as school counselor, which started after the holiday break. But since her old job had ended at the end of November, they had agreed that she could spend the month of December hanging around the school, helping where she could, and getting to know the teachers and students and their parents.

It was the kind of opportunity that existed only in a small town school.

Small towns.

She looked again at the sparkling Christmas decorations, the cheerful, yet dark, store windows, and wondered again how she'd ended up here, because she didn't really think of herself as a small town girl.

A light caught her eye, something a little different, a little warmer than the rest, and she looked across the street, her gaze catching on a cute, weatherbeaten sign in the shape of a candy cane. Then she looked below the sign to the yellow light that had caught her attention.

Behind the counter, a man—impossible to tell his age from where she was in her car—stood at the counter, dumping ingredients into a large mixing bowl. A white apron was tied around his waist, with a picture she couldn't discern, but she guessed probably had something to do with Christmas on the front of it. It was faded and worn, and yet somehow still cheerful and Christmasy, even though she couldn't see the details.

Someone was up early this morning. As early as she was.

Although he hadn't driven from Baltimore. He was happy, content to do his job in an old store in a small town, where he'd probably lived all of his life.

It wasn't something she ever saw for herself, but... somehow the idea of living in a small town didn't seem quite as repulsive as it had through her teen years and college years.

Her roommate, Nelly, had constantly raved about the amazing close-knit, family-like atmosphere of her small town. But Kate had been determined that she would remain a city girl. After all, teaching in an inner city school for an impossibly low wage was one way to give back to her community, wasn't it?

Her car inched down the road, and she lost sight of the man in the window as she pondered that question. It didn't feel like she was giving anything back. The things she was teaching at the inner-city school didn't really help her students at all, and she wasn't allowed to talk about her faith. Not even a word. And yet, she could tell them all kinds of lies about genders and sexuality and despicable things that went against every moral code she might have, and it was perfectly okay. How was that serving her children?

It had become a moral dilemma for her, and then the terrible breakup last Christmas of the engagement that she thought was going to lead to a happily ever after for her had ripped everything out from underneath her, and she had started applying for other jobs in other communities, although... again, she wasn't sure she wanted to be a small town girl.

Somehow, she found herself in a parking lot at a church at the edge of town. She turned around and started driving back through, ostensibly looking for places for rent.

Baltimore's high rents and low wages had left her with very little savings, and she needed someplace cheap and fast.

Her savings would dwindle exceptionally quickly if she had to stay at a hotel for very long. Not to mention, the closest one was forty-five minutes away.

She turned around and tried to justify the second trip through because she needed to find a place to stay, and she might have missed a for-rent sign.

But deep down, she knew it was because the town made her feel like she was curled up in an ugly Christmas sweater, a mug of cocoa in one hand, a fire blazing in the hearth, as she read a good book and the Christmas tree twinkled in the corner beside her.

How did a town give a person a feeling like that? She never felt like that in the city. But she loved the hustle and the bustle and the busyness and the fact that there was always someone awake, and she never felt alone. Weren't small towns lonely? And dead? Boring?

The yellow lights of the candy shop caught her attention again along with the man, still behind the counter, still working, still doing what he always did, she supposed.

This time, she noticed the elaborate candy cane display in the window and the sign that said "Handmade Candy Canes."

Did people actually handmake candy canes?

She didn't even know that was a thing.

But the store just seemed so cozy, the display so blatantly Christmasy, and the man obviously content with his work. He wasn't on his phone, and he didn't even look up as her headlights flashed by.

What would it be like to be so grounded and rooted in one's life?

Kate set the feeling aside. More than likely, small towns were not for her, but it would be a nice change of pace, give her a little bit of something to put on her résumé to beef it up some, for the time when she got her next job at a big school in the city.

And not as an assistant counselor, but as the head counselor.

She told herself she had to familiarize herself with the town, the people, and the things that they did. Now she knew there was a candy cane shop in town, and a man who was up early to get started making something unique.

By the time she rolled through town again, she hadn't seen any for-rent signs, but the place was starting to come to life and dawn had started to break over the top of the eastern foothills.

The Blue Ridge Mountains were to the west, although the town was high enough up that she felt like she was living on one. Maybe they were. She didn't really do a whole lot of research into the topography; she had to admit that she was surprised to see snow in Virginia this early in December. Who would have thought?

Certainly not her, although when her college roommate, Nelly Bushnell, now Nelly McBride, had taken her home for holiday break one year there had been snow the last day, if she remembered correctly. The whole family had gone out and played in it, and Kate had joined in with them, but at the same time she had felt like it was a little... juvenile.

She still had another thirty minutes before she could conceivably show up at the school, and even then she would be early. Parking at the church where she'd turned around twice, she got out of her car, being sure to lock the door since it contained all of her worldly possessions, and then started walking up the street slowly, taking big lungfuls of the mountain-scented air. It felt crisp and cool and somehow cleaner than the air she was used to breathing. Was that a thing?

It had to be in her imagination. Air wasn't cleaner in small towns. Cities had done an outstanding job of becoming more environmentally friendly and Baltimore hardly ever had to deal with smog or anything of the sort anymore.

"Kate!"

Kate turned around at the sound of the female voice. She thought she recognized it, and a smile took over her face as she saw her good friend, Nelly. Now Nelly McBride. Nelly had gotten married over the past year, which had been bittersweet for Kate, since she had also planned a wedding for earlier this year, except last Christmas, her fiancé had called it off. On Christmas Day morning. Of all times.

Shaking those bad memories out of her head, Kate returned Nelly's hug, listening as Nelly introduced her husband, Roland McBride.

"It's good to meet you," she said, shaking the hand that had been offered.

"Nelly always talks about what a great friend you are. Sounds like you guys had some fun times in college."

Kate smiled. Nelly had been a fabulous roommate, kind and considerate, and while she had always been up for a good time, she'd also been a great study partner as well.

"Those were the days," she said with a small smile.

Nelly nodded. "I was so bummed that you weren't able to make it to our wedding."

"I'd had that mission trip scheduled for years, and I didn't want to miss it." Her heart had always been in helping underprivileged people, children especially. But lately she'd begun to wonder if maybe the way she'd been helping ended up not really being much of a help. Giving people things never seemed to make them better. And in fact, she'd seen real life data that had shown that when children were given things instead of having to earn them, it made them worse.

That study was one of the many things that had gotten her thinking and had inspired her to resign her job and apply for other jobs, including the one here in Mistletoe Meadows. That, and the fact that Edward had broken up with her.

"Have you found a place to stay yet?" Nelly asked, her head tilted slightly to one side, her eyes sparkling with joy and happiness.

It was amazing how being with the right person could do that to a person. Nelly just seemed to glow.

Kate pushed down the little frission of jealousy that threatened to steal her peace and happiness.

She was happy. Of course she was. She was starting a new job in a new town. She had been hired over all of the other applicants, and Principal Stevens was excited about the job that they were going to do together.

And so was she.

"No, I haven't. That was part of the reason I was walking around town. I thought maybe I had missed a sign or something. Are there no places for rent here?"

"The market is tight, that's for sure," Roland said, his voice sounding grave and serious.

He and Nelly looked at each other and seemed to nod a bit before Nelly turned to her and said, "But you could stay with us. We're living with Roland's mom right now, and my grandma moved in too. But there's plenty of bedrooms in that big old farmhouse."

Nelly was going to go on, but Kate put a hand up, cutting her off.

"That is so very generous of you, but I couldn't possibly impose on Roland's mother's house."

There was no way she was going to take her up on that offer. A person just didn't do things like that. It was one thing to go home with her for a couple of weeks over the holidays. That had been bad enough, but to move in with newlyweds and the groom's mother? And some other woman? No way.

"Seriously. We'd love to have you. And there's plenty of room in the house."

"If you don't mind my siblings dropping in once in a while. We're all family there. My mom will probably put you to work too."

"I couldn't imagine living there without working. But of course, I would pay rent, except..." She couldn't explain that she had very little money, but it also just went against her sense of what was right. Because she could see that Nelly really wanted her to. Would that be so terrible? Her moving in with Nelly and her husband and his mom and their grandma?

Yeah, they seemed sincere, and maybe things were different here in a small town versus where she grew up in the city, but in Kate's experience, people really didn't want to be imposed upon like that.

So she rebuffed Nelly's efforts to get her to change her mind, firmly saying that she would spend more time hunting for a place to stay.

"Then at least stay with us until you find a place. It would be cheaper than a hotel."

"That's very nice of you. If I don't find a place by the new year, maybe I'll take you up on it."

Nelly looked disappointed, but she nodded.

The new year was a month away; surely she would find a place by then.

"If I can't get you to stay, at least come for supper tonight," Nelly said, smiling and giving her an appealing look.

She had already said no to the offer of lodging; she could hardly turn down supper. Although, there was still that part of her that didn't want to impose.

"You're not going to be putting anyone out. There's always plenty of food. No one's going to cook anything different if you come. There's just... friendly faces and hearty food." Roland didn't seem like he was begging her, but he was simply laying out the facts. Did he really not mind people descending on his house?

"You talked me into it," she said, still unable to believe that it wouldn't be an imposition. At the very least, they would have more dishes to do.

"Awesome. We'll see you tonight at six. Does that work?" Nelly said, her eyes shining like Kate had just given her a hundred-dollar bill, rather than an agreement to eat supper with her. Maybe Kate was looking at it all wrong.

She tucked that thought away for later. It was possible that she was mistaken, although she had been raised to give other people a wide berth and respect their privacy and family. Again she thought that maybe it was the difference between growing up in the city and growing up in a small town.

After a little bit more small talk, they parted ways, with Kate going back to her car and heading toward the school.

As she passed by the candy cane shop one more time, she glanced in the window and saw a little girl staring silently at the man, who appeared to be talking.

Other shops were open on the street now, and the town had, if not come to life, at least started to wake up.

Maybe that little girl would be at school in a bit, and perhaps Kate would meet her, along with all the other children.

It was going to be a big difference from the school that she had been at, a much smaller student population. Less than a quarter of what it had been at the inner city school where she had worked.

In one way, she was looking forward to possibly knowing the name of every child, which Principal Stevens had assured her every teacher and administrator knew.

Kate somehow found that exciting and unbelievable at the same time.

Regardless, a little thrill of excitement went through her, for the change if nothing else, as she got in her car and headed toward the school.

Chapter Two

Jack Henderson glanced at the timer and then picked up one of the strings of hard candy that he had set to cool in the pan on the counter.

"Did you finish getting all of your homework together?" he asked his daughter, a rhetorical question since he knew she would not answer him, as he picked up the candy and began rolling it between his hands.

What had been strange and foreign ten years prior now came as easily as brushing his teeth or driving his tractor.

Without thinking about it, his hands expertly shaped the cooling candy into a perfect candy cane shape.

He looked over his shoulder, lifting a brow at his daughter, Lilly.

She was waiting for his glance, and she nodded one time, her head going up and down seriously, her eyes grave and serious.

"And everything else is ready to go?" he asked, waiting for her nod before he turned back to the candy.

She hadn't spoken a word since her mother had died three years prior. At this point, Jack had despaired of ever hearing her speak again.

They'd developed a rhythm, an easy camaraderie, and while it was a little bit harder than it might have been had she been able to speak, they'd gotten along fine.

It wasn't that she wasn't able to speak. The doctors told him there was nothing physically wrong. It was that she had chosen not to.

Jack felt guilt grip his insides, the way it always did when it came to his daughter. Was he failing her? Had he done everything he could? He knew he wasn't a very good mother, but he had been doing the best job he could at being the best daddy he could as well. On top of that, he'd been trying to keep the candy shop afloat, so that someday Lilly would inherit it—what had been her mother's family's legacy. Lilly would be the seventh generation of candy cane makers, and it was a heritage that the entire family had been proud of.

It had been exceptionally important to Lauren that Lilly be schooled in everything candy.

Jack had neglected his farm and the duties there, dumping them all on his brother, Bryan, in order to keep Lauren's dream alive and viable. But financial constraints were pressing horrendously down, and he wasn't sure how much longer the shop could stay afloat.

As if on cue, Jack lifted his eyes and saw two men in business suits walking by the front window.

They were peering in with interest, the way they had every morning for the last three days.

He tried to lift one corner of his mouth and nod his head in friendly greeting, although his interior felt anything but friendly. He wanted to tell the men to go find another town to open up their chain store in.

But a chain store in the general area would employ over one hundred people, plus delivery personnel, and probably Mistletoe Meadows could afford to hire more police and other government workers, and increase tax revenue, build a bigger school, just... a chain store would snowball economic development in a massively great and amazing way.

But it would probably, almost certainly, drive Jack and his candy cane creations out of business, destroying Lauren's dream and keeping Lilly from ever being able to step into the shoes of her ancestors.

He heard water running and turned to see Lilly washing her hands. She already had a hair cap on, and he almost told her to stop.

A quick glance at the clock on the wall told him that they only had twenty minutes before it was time for him to take her to school, and she didn't have time to help him.

But he kept his mouth closed. She loved helping, and he wanted to encourage it. Even if it did make things harder for him, since when she was younger, teaching her had also included ruined batches of candy.

Now, she was almost as good as he was at rolling the candy and shaping it into candy canes. Still, it added a little bit of stress, because she was no longer ready to walk out the door.

He did not allow her to see those thoughts, but instead smiled encouragingly at her as she came over, standing beside him and picking up one of the ropes of candy.

She knew as well as he did how imperative it was that they get the candy formed before it cooled so much that it was no longer pliable.

She pointed to the blue-colored candy and looked up and smiled at him.

"I know. Blueberry is your favorite too."

That was how he had met his wife. He had been delivering blueberries to their store, since they were trying to source local ingredients for their candy. His family farm had a ten-acre plot of blueberries, and they'd been more than happy to have some of them made into candy and sold locally.

He and his brother had been taking the farm over from their dad, and that's how he had met Lauren, when she had greeted him at the back door and helped him unload the delivery.

He smiled a little at the memory. But it was bittersweet, since Lauren was no longer with him. Sometimes it annoyed him that she had left him with all the work, all the pressure, and hadn't at least told him that keeping up the family farm was just as important as making sure there was a candy shop for their daughter to inherit someday.

He was pretty sure that's the way Lauren would feel, but... she had never said, and he had never thought to ask. She had worked at the shop, and he had left the farm in order to help her, and they had been fine for years and years, until... Lauren's untimely death from an aneurysm while she was showering.

Her parents had come back for the funeral, of course, but neither one of them had been interested in the candy shop. Lauren's grandmother had taught her pretty much everything she knew, and Lauren had loved every second of it.

He felt a touch on his side and looked down to see Lilly's elbow touching his waist.

That was how she got his attention since she knew better than to use her fingers to touch, since they had been washed and she now had gloves on.

She had just formed her third candy cane, and his hands had stilled around his. It was hardening in his hand, even as he looked at her.

"I'm sorry. I was just thinking."

Her brows raised, and he knew she was asking what he was thinking about.

"Nothing really. Just... Christmas is coming, and I need to figure out what in the world I'm going to get my daughter. She hasn't made me a list yet." He lifted his brows and gave her a stern look, but kind and loving as well.

Lilly shook her head and turned away from him, pulling the gloves off her hands.

He didn't need to tell her that the shop was struggling. Somehow she knew. He had tried to protect her from those things, even though he wasn't sure that that was really what a father should do. Maybe she should know. After all, if she was going to be a part of the business eventually, she'd need to figure it out. But, considering that she was just in elementary school, it was too much for her small shoulders.

"Are you going to be in the Christmas play this year?" he asked.

She nodded, tossing her gloves in the trash.

He finished putting the last touch on his candy cane and then snapped his gloves off as well. They would have just enough time to head out the back door and get in the car to get to school on time.

Maybe Jack underestimated that just a bit, since the bell rang as Lilly stepped out on the sidewalk.

Knowing that he would need to write her a note, he offered her his hand, and they walked up the sidewalk together toward the principal's office.

This had happened more times than Jack cared to admit. Again, he had to admit he was a little upset with Lauren for dying on him, which he knew made absolutely no sense, but it was the way he felt. After all, as a single dad, trying to keep the candy shop afloat and deal with Lilly, who wasn't hard but was still a child and needed him, and in his spare time, trying to help his brother on the farm and keep that going as well—that was his backup if the candy shop didn't make it. And it was his dream, what he enjoyed.

"We're going to talk to Principal Stevens before you go to your classroom. I'll make sure that he knows it's my fault that you were late."

Lilly squeezed his hand but didn't say anything.

Maybe he was wrong, but he kind of thought that his daughter was annoyed with him, wanting him to be a better dad, wanting more out of him.

Was that just his imagination?

He opened the front door and held it while Lilly walked through.

She waited to take his hand again, which made him feel good. Maybe she wasn't terribly upset with him after all.

The principal's office was in the main hallway, right near the nurse's office and the counselor's office, which was empty. The previous counselor had left the week before, and from what he understood from Principal Stevens, the new one wasn't going to start until the new year, per her contract.

He remembered Principal Stevens saying something about the person coming and hanging around the school just to get to know everyone before she started her official duties. He hoped this counselor would be a little better than the last one and take an interest in Lilly somehow.

Or at least give Jack some better pointers of what he could do, beyond waiting and seeing, which was the solution of the last counselor.

"Good morning, Jack," Principal Stevens said, as he strode to the entrance of his doorway, like they were catching him on his way out.

"Good morning. I'm sorry; we stepped in as the bell rang, so I knew that meant I needed to make a trip here to make sure Lilly got checked in okay."

"Yeah, we've got her," Mr. Stevens said, and he didn't seem to have any judgment on his face. Maybe he truly did think that Jack was doing the best he could. Maybe he wasn't judging. Maybe it was just Jack's imagination that everyone thought he should be doing better.

"Lilly, you go on to your classroom. Your dad and I will take care of this. I saw you guys pulling in, and I messaged your teacher. She's expecting you."

Lilly nodded, and then her sweet blue eyes looked up at her dad.

Jack's heart melted as he knelt on one knee and gave her a hug. Her little arms wrapped around his neck, and she squeezed him back tightly. She was only seven, but it felt like she was growing up way too fast.

"You'll be good," he said, ruffling her hair affectionately as she grinned at him. And then she turned around, her backpack dwarfing her skinny little body as she walked confidently down the hall toward her classroom.

Jack straightened, and he and Mr. Stevens watched Lilly go.

Mr. Stevens must have been waiting for her to be out of earshot, because as soon as she turned the corner, he turned to Jack and said, "Our new counselor is starting after Christmas. I know I told you that."

"Yeah."

"I've already discussed Lilly with her, since she arrived early this morning." Mr. Stevens paused, and then in a rare show of annoyance, he said, "She has a better work ethic than the last counselor, who only seemed to show up for work in order to collect her paycheck."

"It's a bad career choice if a person only wants a paycheck," Jack said, although he had already surmised as much from the previous counselor. He supposed he really didn't know of any job where a person should just show up. If they couldn't put their heart and soul into their work, why didn't they just find something else where they could?

But he knew the answer to that was a lot more complicated than the question would make it seem. And he didn't have time to solve the world's problems. He had enough of his own.

Still, he wanted to live his life for the glory of the Lord, and one way to do that was to do his very best at everything he did, including his job. Even if making candy wasn't exactly what he had dreamed of doing when he was a kid, or even when he was an adult. But it seemed to be the path that God had laid out for him, and regardless of what he wanted, he needed to do what he knew was right.

"I'm sorry I can't introduce you this morning. She's already off checking in on the kindergartners. She said she would start with the youngest first and work her way up."

"Well, when she gets to the third grade, she'll meet Lilly."

"Yes. I don't expect her to be there until tomorrow."

Jack nodded. Hopefully this counselor would be a little better than the last one, although he'd done everything he could for Lilly. He couldn't imagine that a counselor would make much difference. The little girl had just been through so much trauma, losing her mother and having to learn to deal with him. He wasn't much of a dad, at least most of the time he didn't feel like it.

And then this summer she'd been sick, and spent so much time in the hospital. Almost two weeks. Whatever progress they had made before that seemed to be totally erased.

"I look forward to meeting her," Jack said, as he held his hand out, and Mr. Stevens shook it.

He did look forward to meeting the new counselor, but he wasn't holding his breath that anything was going to change.

Chapter Three

Kate parked her still fully loaded car in the driveway of Roland and Nelly's house.

It was a huge old farmhouse, gorgeous in that way of years gone by, where no expense had been spared for the trim and the detail work on the front porch that wrapped around the side of the house like a hug.

Christmas decorations brightened the front of it even more, with a pretty green wreath and sparkling red decorations hung on the front door.

It was obvious the family used the back door, though, and that was where Kate headed as she got out of her car.

She felt like she should be bringing something, a loaf of homemade bread or something, but she'd gotten herself settled in her hotel room and then scoured the internet looking for places she could schedule an appointment to go see, so she could get something to rent as soon as possible.

She hadn't expected to have this much trouble.

She'd been busy wrapping things up at the end of her tenure in Baltimore, and while she had checked out a few places, she hadn't realized it was going to be so difficult. Obviously, she should have been more prepared. But she had been busy preparing her successor to take over her job.

Walking up the back steps, where Christmas lights twinkled on the banister and a sweet nativity display sat sheltered in a corner, she knocked on the back door and tried to tamp down her nerves.

Nelly was one of the nicest people she knew. And she remembered the McBride family as super warm and welcoming from when she'd met them years ago.

"Hello!" an older woman said as she opened the door.

"You must be Mrs. McBride," Kate said, offering her hand and a gentle smile.

"I sure am, Kate. It's been years since you visited our town with Nelly, but you've not changed that much," Mrs. McBride said, ignoring her outstretched hand and instead wrapping cinnamon-scented arms around her and squeezing tightly.

Somehow, the hug felt like home and family, and memories of childhood, warm and soft, floated through Kate's mind. She didn't have a whole lot of good ones, but hugging this woman brought them all to the surface.

"You can call me Marjorie. And you are welcome to come on in and make yourself at home," Marjorie said, pulling the door open further and stepping back so Kate could walk in.

"Kate!" Nelly said, hurrying over. "I'm so glad you could come. I know I promised you that we weren't going to make anything special, but Marjorie insisted on whipping up her homemade baked mac and cheese." Nelly lowered her voice and waggled her eyebrows. "It is so good."

Kate laughed at Nelly's overdramatization. "It sounds like it is," she said. Baked mac and cheese? When was the last time she had that? All of her friends from Baltimore were on low-carb diets. Mac and cheese was definitely on the do-not-eat list. Ever.

Kate really hadn't jumped on that bandwagon exactly, but it was just easier to go along to get along, and she definitely ate fewer carbs than she used to. Still, baked mac and cheese, along with the cozy interior of the farmhouse—pale blue kitchen cabinets, gray tile floor, and white granite countertops along with a butcher block-topped bar—made the place feel warm and cozy. Of course, there was a sprig of mistletoe above the door, greenery in the windows, along with lighted candles, and a scented candle burning on the mantle.

This place could have come out of a Norman Rockwell painting, especially combined with the laughter and good-natured teasing of the adults.

"You already know my husband, and I assume Mom introduced herself."

Kate nodded. "She sure did," she said, remembering the hug that Marjorie had greeted her with.

"This is my sister-in-law, Isadora. She lives here with her three kids. I'm sure you'll see them in school," Nelly said, as a beautiful but sad-eyed woman walked into the kitchen.

"It's so nice to meet you. You're the new counselor, right?"

"Yes. I start after the Christmas break, but Principal Stevens and the school board agreed that I could float around for the month of December, getting to know the children and the teachers."

She wasn't making any money, which was another reason why she had to watch her pennies. Somehow she'd misjudged—she had thought her start date was going to be the beginning of December, but the school district had decided to do some renovations to the counselor's room, and the contract they had offered her began in January.

It was fine by Kate; it would be much better for the children and for her to get used to things.

"I can't believe how different things are here," she said. And it wasn't just the school.

"You spent the day at the school already?" Isadora asked, walking to the sink and washing her hands.

"Yes. There's so much to learn. But there aren't nearly as many kids in this school as there were at my old one, so I'm pretty confident that I'm going to be able to learn everyone's name."

"That's one of the very nice things about small schools," Nelly said.

She looked around and then said to Marjorie, who was mashing the potatoes, "What can I do to help?"

Isadora had started chopping tomatoes on the cutting board, with a bowl of greens sitting beside her, and Nelly had opened the oven door and was pulling out a delicious-smelling casserole.

"If you don't mind taking the baked chicken that I have there on the sheet and putting it in that bowl, I think everything will be ready."

Kate, happy to have a job, grabbed the tongs that were sitting beside the chicken and started lifting it in, listening as laughter and joking went on behind her.

Isadora had instructed the children to set the table, and Nelly had mentioned that another sibling was going to come for dessert. Apparently that family did therapy, and the mom had a client.

Everything seemed so happy and cozy, and while Kate felt right at home, there was also a little bit of sadness because this was the kind of family she'd missed out on growing up.

Both of her parents had been professionals, and most of their suppers had consisted of takeout, or for a while, her mom had hired a meal service.

But this camaraderie around the kitchen where everybody was helping was new and... compelling.

Somehow everything was ready at the same time, and Kate carried her chicken in and sat down beside Nelly and Marjorie, with Isadora across the table from her.

To her surprise, everyone bowed their heads and said grace before the meal. Normally, Kate said a quiet grace to herself, but how long had it been since she'd been in a home that took the time to thank the Lord out loud?

Even when she'd been growing up, her parents, although they

had been regular church attendees—going two or three times a month—had not said grace before their meals.

Everyone said, "Amen," and then began to pass the food.

Kate made an extra effort to learn the names of the children and to use them in conversation. They were included at the table as naturally as breathing, and it was obvious all the adults adored them.

"So where did you grow up, Kate?" Marjorie said with a smile and genuine curiosity, spoken like someone who cared. "I remember you coming home with Nelly when she came home from college one year. I saw you at church a couple of times, I believe."

"Good memory," Kate said, impressed. She had a vague memory of an older woman who'd been especially nice, but she couldn't remember whether it was Marjorie or not.

"I grew up in Maryland, near the shore. The Baltimore area, although I didn't live in the city. We lived in the suburbs until I began teaching in the city after college."

"That's nice. Inner city school?" Marjorie asked, looking impressed.

Kate smiled to herself. She'd always wanted to give back to the community, and she'd thought teaching at an inner-city school for a lower salary would be a good way. It hadn't really turned out that way, though.

"Yes, it was. Those kids just need so much."

"It's great that they have people like you who are willing to make the sacrifice to help them."

"So many teachers are willing to make the sacrifice, but we're hamstrung by red tape and politics."

She didn't want to turn the conversation into a political discussion, although she had plenty to say about it. She was here with this family at this table enjoying their generosity and didn't want to turn the dinner table conversation into an argument. "But it was very rewarding in a lot of different ways. I'll definitely miss the children there."

She wouldn't miss the administration at all, and walking into this town and this home felt so much different than the impersonal and almost clinical way the inner city school felt. Not to mention, while she was surrounded by people, she had never felt more alone.

Maybe that was her fault somehow, although she did go out with her friends.

Perhaps it was just a relic of Edward breaking up with her.

"I think you'll find a lot of kids at our school will appreciate you being here," Isadora said easily, as though she also wanted to avoid the political discussion.

She couldn't talk to them about the specific children that Principal Stevens had talked to her about that day, although one little girl—she couldn't remember her name—had been mute since her mother died. That had intrigued Kate. Hopefully she was going to meet the little girl tomorrow when she visited the third-grade classroom.

"Principal Stevens had a lot to say about the children. And it does sound like I could be useful here."

"In more ways than one," Nelly said with a secretive smile.

Kate smiled back, but inside she was curious. What in the world could Nelly mean?

Nelly had been correct about the mac and cheese. It was the best that she had ever had. And that was saying something, because she had had a lot of mac and cheese growing up. But this was warm and savory and creamy and delicious, and when the container got passed around for a second time, she found herself taking another scoop. She had planned to skip dessert, but when the apple pie came around, she took a slice of that as well.

"I'm not going to be able to eat here very often. My waistline won't allow it," she joked as they cleared off the table, and Nelly told her she'd need to come back.

"You just need to do a lot more exercising," Nelly said with a laugh.

"Or you can call it middle-aged spread, which is what I do,"

Isadora said, although as Kate looked at Isadora, she didn't really see any spread, middle-aged or not. Although she did see dark circles around the woman's eyes, and if she remembered correctly, Nelly had told her that Isadora's husband had cheated on her and left her and her three children.

Gilbert and Summer had arrived with their children. Apparently Summer was a licensed equine therapist, and Kate made a note that she wanted to see if she could talk to Summer and see if perhaps they could work with each other. She didn't know exactly what she was going to run into at the school, but it wouldn't hurt to have an idea of what Summer offered in mind as she thought about the children.

Isadora soon took her kids into the living room and had them sit down to do their homework. Interestingly, Gilbert and Summer's kids had brought their homework as well, and soon the cousins were all sitting at the table, laughing but also working.

How nice it would be to have a ready-made study group, Kate thought to herself as she glanced in and saw Marjorie helping one of the girls with her homework, and Isadora bent over another helping with reading. Roland and Gilbert were standing around the table too.

"I had hoped to have a chance to talk to you," Kate said to Summer, who was rinsing off the dishes and putting them in the dishwasher.

"Oh?" Summer said, looking up in a friendly manner.

"Yes. I'm going to be the new counselor at the school, and I heard you do equine therapy."

"I do. It sounds like you and I might have a lot to talk about."

"You work with children?"

"Almost exclusively. Sometimes I do family counseling therapy, but almost always it's children. It's not that I'm not open to adults; it's just... horses seem to relate to children, and children seem to relate to horses the best."

"I think as we get to be adults, we start to be scared of things that didn't used to bother us at all."

"You could be right about that," Summer said with a laugh.

She and Summer talked for a bit about different ways that they could help each other with their therapy, while Nelly cleared off the tables and counters and wiped them down.

"I look forward to working with you," Summer said, and then she nodded toward the table. "I probably better go and make sure that my children are actually getting their schoolwork done."

"Spoken like a wonderful mother," Kate said.

She was just about ready to offer to help when Nelly touched her arm. "I was hoping I could have a word with you, if you don't mind?"

"Not at all," Kate said, her brow furrowing, wondering what in the world Nelly wanted.

"Can we step out on the porch?"

"Sure," Kate said.

Her jacket had been hung on a peg by the door, and she grabbed it as they walked out quietly. She didn't think any of the kids noticed, although she saw Marjorie glancing up to see what was going on.

That was when she noticed the deep shadows around Marjorie's eyes and the slight droop of her eyelids. Like she was exhausted.

She wondered if anyone else had noticed.

"I've been watching for you two to make your move," a deep voice said, as the door opened behind Kate and Roland slipped out.

"I figured you would see us," Nelly said with a laugh.

So both Roland and Nelly wanted to talk to her?

She wasn't sure exactly what that meant, but she was definitely curious now.

"So..." Roland looked at Nelly.

"You go ahead."

"This was your idea," Roland said.

"You're the leader."

"Why do you throw that up every time there's some kind of question about who needs to go first?"

"Because you throw it up every time you want to go first," Nelly said, and they laughed together.

Watching the interplay between the two of them made Kate

realize that it was probably a good thing that she and Edward had broken up. They hadn't had this kind of easy-going banter between the two of them. In fact, if she were being perfectly honest, she didn't really enjoy being with him that much. It was just the idea that her biological clock was ticking and she wanted children. She wanted a family. She wanted what she had just experienced in this house at the McBride supper table. And in order to have that, she knew she needed to get married.

Edward had been a good choice on the surface anyway. The problem was, he didn't seem to like her any more than she liked him.

"So do you remember when I told you about how Roland and I have something that we do, and it's absolutely top secret."

"You said something about being like a Secret Santa? As long as it's not illegal, my job requires that I keep secrets, so I'm pretty good at it."

She had wanted to talk about specific children at the dinner table, but she knew she wasn't able to. And even though she probably could have mentioned names and asked about the kids, and that wouldn't have been considered breaking the protocol of her job, especially since she hadn't even been officially hired, she just liked to use an abundance of caution. After all, if someone was considering working with her for any kind of counseling they needed, she would appreciate them being discreet and tight-lipped about her and her problems.

Not that she'd ever gone to a counselor, which was maybe odd, considering that she was one.

"Nothing illegal. My wife hasn't dragged me into a life of crime yet," Roland said with a raised brow at his wife and a look that could only be described as adoration.

It gave Kate a little shock of jealousy.

She tried to shove it aside. She was happy for her friend, and she definitely did not want anything to happen to their relationship, but she wouldn't mind having a relationship like that for herself.

But those kinds of relationships only came around once in a

lifetime. Or at least that's what she thought. And sometimes they didn't come around at all. Maybe she wouldn't be one of the lucky ones.

Maybe it wasn't luck.

Probably not. Probably it had a lot to do with the Lord.

God? Is it too much to ask for me to have something like that?

"Yes. I've mentioned before that Roland and I are involved with the Secret Saints, which is basically a Secret Santa for the town of Mistletoe Meadows."

"You help someone who goes around giving gifts to people anonymously?" Kate said, remembering that they'd talked about it the previous year. But she had been blindsided by her fiance breaking up with her on Christmas Day, and she really hadn't thought about the Secret Saint thing since.

"Exactly. There is a vast network of people who are willing to donate, and people that they can talk to who will help provide gifts and such. Although, most of them do not know who the actual Secret Saint actually is."

"That's really awesome," Kate said, loving the idea, although she was kind of confused as to what that had to do with her. Why were they telling her?

"Considering that you'll be working with a lot of children whose families might need a hand, and also you might have some extra time on your hands as you get to know people, we thought you might be interested in keeping an ear out."

"Your job is perfect for knowing who might need help. Because that's a big part of the equation. Not just gathering gifts and figuring out things they can do to help people, but knowing who needs the help."

"Oh. I see."

"Basically, we're recruiting you to become a part of the Secret Saint network. Would you be interested?" Nelly just flat out asked her, and Kate appreciated her directness. That was part of the reason they'd always been good friends.

"I would love to." She knew she should probably say "I'll pray about it," or "Let me think about it," or at least play hard to get a little bit, but she had loved the idea from the moment they said it, and this totally played to every desire she had to be a help to people who needed her.

"Although, I'd really like to only help people who actually need it. Sometimes you see things like this happening, and people get free stuff just because... the people who are giving it out don't know anyone else to give it to. Do you know what I mean?" She'd seen a lot of that in the inner city—the same people getting more and more and more, and never learning how to do for themselves.

Unfortunately, she didn't really have a solution to the problem. When there was a need, she just couldn't help herself from wanting to be able to help with it. She supposed there were a lot of other people like that.

"I told you she would want to," Nelly said to Roland.

"You were right, dear," Roland said with an affectionate eye roll.

"Is there a protocol for anything?" Kate asked.

"No. What we do is we just keep our eyes and ears open for people who might need help, and then we keep our eyes and ears open for people who can give help, and we try to match things up. You can come to us with your information and we'll pass it along to the folks who need to know. We just wait for our opportunity, gather supplies, and then we let the right people know."

"Nice."

"Speaking of, we have some supplies for someone who's been going through a very difficult time for the last three years, but especially the last six months."

"All right," Kate said slowly.

"And we were hoping that you would be able to deliver them tonight on your way home."

"Sure. I don't know the area very well—"

"It's right in the middle of town. If you've driven through it, you've gone by the candy cane shop."

"Yes. It looks so quaint and nostalgic. I think there might have even been a penny candy display in the store, although I didn't walk in."

"There is. And there is still candy for a penny."

"That's neat," she said. She remembered way back when she was really small, visiting her grandmother and going to an old-fashioned candy store that still had penny candy. It had been fun and different, although she'd only ever gone once.

"We have some supplies that we need you to drop off there. You can just put them right in front of his door. Jack will see them tomorrow when he opens."

"Aren't you afraid someone's going to steal them?"

"No. This is Mistletoe Meadows, not Baltimore. The town will be dead until tomorrow morning, and Jack gets up before anyone else in town."

"I don't know of anyone who works harder than Jack does," Roland said, and although his eyes were still crinkled, his tone and face were serious.

"All right." Kate nodded. "Just let me know what you need me to drop off, and I'll do it."

"Actually, if you don't mind, Roland can put the things in your car."

"I don't mind at all. There's a little bit of room in the front passenger seat. The rest of it is packed with all my stuff."

"Have you found a place to live yet?" Nelly asked, sounding concerned.

"Not yet, but I'm going to," Kate said, remembering that they had offered to allow her to stay there, and after seeing everyone interacting tonight, she was tempted. But she just couldn't bring herself to impose.

"If you change your mind about my offer..." Nelly smiled, and Kate shook her head.

"I'll say something if I need it." But she hoped she wouldn't. She really needed to knuckle down and find a place. She couldn't continue to stay in a hotel, but she absolutely couldn't impose on the McBrides anymore.

"I'll tell you what, I'll stop nagging you to come live with us if you at least agree to eat with us at least five nights a week," Nelly lifted her brows.

"Six," Roland said.

Kate laughed.

"I'll try. Tell you what, I will not eat alone. I will come here, unless I have someone else to eat with. Does that sound okay?"

"Sure does. Let's go back in and talk to everyone for a bit while Roland puts the things in your car."

"Sounds good. If you don't mind helping me go over the kids' names again. That will be six children that I won't have to learn at school. That'll be my homework for the night."

They laughed as Nelly put her arm through Kate's, and they walked in the door.

Chapter Four

It turned out that Kate and Summer got into a huge discussion about counseling and therapy and the children that they could help, and it was midnight until Kate left the McBride's house, with Summer beside her, since she was dropping Summer off at home, because Gilbert had taken the children home hours ago to get them to bed at a decent time.

"Thanks so much for talking to me. It's so nice to find someone else who is as concerned about the children as I am, and not just concerned about making ourselves feel good by doing 'good deeds,'" she said, using her fingers to make air quotes.

"We just want to throw money at people, or things at them, when in reality, that just patches the problem. It's the old 'Give a man a fish or teach him to fish' adage, which has a lot of truth to it." Summer nodded her head as she spoke, and Kate had to agree. They'd spent the evening talking about how they could equip the children to deal with their issues, rather than just putting a band-aid on them, teaching them to walk through the issues, facing them, and not telling them that it wasn't fair or wasn't right.

Kate didn't think for one second that she had everything figured out, but she did know a lot of the things that were happening in the city schools weren't working. More money wasn't the answer. And more of the same wasn't the answer either, since things had gotten worse, not better.

Summer got out of the car at the farm, promising to stay in touch. Kate pulled out of the driveway feeling like she'd made a new friend.

As she carefully set the packages back down on the front seat and shut the door, Kate remembered that she had promised Nelly that she would drop those things off at the candy cane shop for... what did she call it? The secret saints?

Interesting, how in one evening she could go from wondering what her purpose was to feeling like maybe she'd found it with finding a kindred spirit in Summer, and the idea that she could help people who actually needed it anonymously, in the town where she was planted.

As she drove back through Mistletoe Meadows on her way to the hotel, she kept an eye out for for-rent signs, but the town was dark and quiet.

Except for the warm yellow light in the window of the candy cane shop.

To her surprise, the man, Jack, was still working at the counter. His shoulders moved along with his arms as Kate assumed he was rolling out candy canes.

They looked like big ones, with his huge movements, and Kate found herself not only wondering what the candy canes were for, but wondering about the man himself. What hard times had Nelly been talking about?

She'd only seen one girl, although she remembered Principal Stevens saying that the girl could use therapy. She was mute, but by choice, not by any kind of problem that medical professionals could figure out.

What would cause a child to voluntarily become mute?

Most little girls loved to chatter on. Actually, even boys that age loved to chatter and talk, at least for the purpose of getting what they wanted.

How did that affect the dynamic the little girl had with her father? Was there something medical professionals hadn't seen? Or was the child just so traumatized that she was unable to remember how to talk?

Kate made a mental note to herself to try to look things up and see if she could find anything out. This was her home now, and she wanted to do everything she could for the citizens here.

Since the light was on, she drove slowly down the street and parked at the church where she'd turned around before. Grabbing the bags from the front seat, she slipped quietly down the sidewalk, careful not to allow her feet to make any sound.

Feeling unaccountably nervous—after all, she wasn't doing anything wrong—she also contained the sliver of excitement that moved down her back as she slipped through the shadows, making sure she was doing everything she could to not be seen or heard. After all, she didn't want to blow her identity on her very first secret saint drop-off.

From what Roland and Nelly had said, there could be many more. And they had talked about how important it was to remain anonymous. She was all about that. And they were correct that her position as counselor was perfect for her to learn about people who could use help.

She made it to the front of the candy cane shop, unable to not look in the window and admire the intricate display of candy canes. Even more amazing was the fact that they were all handmade. Wow. It flabbergasted her. It also made her wonder how someone could make a living selling handmade candy canes, especially in a town the size of Mistletoe Meadows.

Somehow she found herself drawn to Jack, wanting to know more about him, but she slipped the bags off of her arm and dropped them in front of the door, turning immediately and hurrying back up the sidewalk.

She didn't even glance in the window to see if Jack had heard anything unusual.

But she was smiling as she got in her car. Even if she didn't have a place to stay and didn't know exactly what the future held, she found herself feeling satisfied and content in ways she hadn't for a very long time.

Chapter Five

"All right, children, take out your math books and go to page 57," Miss Jones stood at the front of the classroom, pulling out a marker for the whiteboard while waiting for the children to follow her instructions.

Kate stood at the back of the classroom, unobtrusively observing. She found her eyes kept being drawn back to Lilly, who sat in the second seat from the front, following her teacher's directions precisely.

The child was excellent. Not a troublemaker at all. Although Kate had not expected her to be. She seemed happy too. Not sad or morose or unwilling to be involved in whatever was going on in the classroom. It wouldn't have shocked Kate had that been the case. After all, the trauma that she had been through might have caused her not to talk because she was depressed.

But Lilly didn't seem depressed.

She carefully observed as the teacher went over the homework from the night before, calling on various children to answer questions.

When it was Lilly's turn, Lilly rose from her seat and went to the whiteboard with her paper, writing the answer on the board without asking permission, as though that had been the protocol.

Everyone seemed completely at ease with that, like it was normal and they were used to it.

"That is correct, Lilly. Thirty-two." Miss Jones looked over the classroom. "Did everybody get that one right?"

Heads nodded, and Miss Jones said, "Very good, Lilly. That one was difficult."

Lilly smiled, put the marker down, and went back to her seat.

There was still a little grin along her mouth as though she were proud that she had gotten such a difficult problem correct.

Miss Jones began explaining it for the kids who didn't get it, and Kate allowed her words to wash over her while she continued to watch Lilly.

The child took her seat and then paid attention to the teacher.

Losing her mother had to have been a very difficult thing for her to go through, but maybe there was something else involved. Some other reason why she wasn't talking. Could there be?

Or maybe she just needed some help to work through whatever it was that she was hanging onto.

Kate rolled those ideas around in her head as the day progressed.

It was the last class of the day, and the kids were soon getting ready to go.

Miss Jones had given them five minutes of free time to talk to their friends before the end of school, and she came back and stood beside Kate.

"What did you think?" she asked with a smile. "Anything strike you?"

"I love Tyler's sense of humor. He tries so hard to be good, but it's just tough for him to sit still."

"Yeah. There have been a couple of days where it's been a real struggle. Once he actually wiggled himself onto the desk, and I had to remind him that he had to stay in his seat. You should have seen the look of surprise on his face when he realized he was actually on his desk. I don't think he even knew." Miss Jones laughed.

"My goodness. But it sounds to me like that's just a matter of too much energy, and not a discipline problem."

"No. Tyler is a good kid. And you can tell a lot by the way a child treats other children. He is very considerate and kind."

"That was the impression I got too," Kate said honestly. Tyler had struck her as someone with a huge sense of humor. He was probably going to grow up to be the class clown, although it was possible he would be the valedictorian too. He was very intelligent. He just needed to get his limbs under control.

"What did you think about Lilly?" Miss Jones asked, lowering her voice a notch as she stood shoulder to shoulder with Kate, looking out over the classroom.

All the kids were getting their things together and chattering with each other. Lilly was a little off by herself, slowly putting her math textbook into her book bag. It was pink and, interestingly, had candy canes on it.

Did Lilly like candy canes? Or was it because her family had the shop and she had no choice about what kind of backpack she was going to have?

The question was interesting, and Kate filed it away to ask later, if she ever got a chance.

"I can't quite put my finger on what it is about her that draws me. She seems very smart."

"She's exceptionally intelligent, but... I just don't think she's working to her ability. She's at the lower end of the class, and I really feel like she should be much higher."

"She seems to be doing well in math."

"She's just average, maybe slightly below. But it's reading where she really is having problems. She really struggles, and she doesn't write anything at all."

"I thought that was how she communicated?"

"Numbers. She writes numbers really well. But not sentences.

Words maybe. Her dad has taught her some hand gestures, and they seem to communicate that way some. But I don't know."

"She would definitely be a good candidate for counseling. Do you think her father would agree to it?"

"She doesn't have a mother."

"Divorce?" Kate asked, knowing that it might have been a little bit of a personal question, but it was something that she was going to need to know if she was going to counsel Lilly.

"She passed away."

"I see."

That made things even harder. "I think she was in the hospital some this summer too," Miss Jones's voice continued to be low and soft.

"I'll definitely want to get some information on her and see if her dad will allow her to spend some time with me."

"He should be here. He always comes to the classroom to pick her up. She doesn't ride the bus like the rest of the children."

"Is he overprotective?" That could be part of the problem. If she had never been allowed to do anything for herself, maybe speaking just followed in line with everything else.

"I don't think so. He's just a single dad doing his best." Miss Jones didn't elaborate, and she soon walked away, helping children who needed her, while Kate continued to stand in the back observing.

"All right, children. It's time to line up for the bus. Those of you whose parents are going to pick you up, don't leave. Remember you cannot leave until I give you permission." Miss Jones sounded like she'd said that a million times as the children moved to do what she asked.

Kate shifted as several parents came to the door—they were mothers. Several mothers came through the door, and their children ran over to them, still at the age where they loved seeing their parents in school.

She was still smiling over that when she glanced at Lilly, who was watching the door intently. Kate didn't have to see movement out of her peripheral vision to know that Lilly's father had arrived. Lilly's face lit up, and she grabbed her bag and speed-walked over to the door of the classroom.

He bent down and gathered his daughter into his arms, the movement natural, like that was the way he always greeted her. She hugged him like they'd been separated for years instead of a few hours.

Maybe that was it. Maybe she was afraid of being abandoned again; maybe she saw her mother as abandoning her and was afraid she would be abandoned again.

She looked a lot different now that her father was there—more relaxed, her shoulders not nearly as tight. Kate hadn't even noticed that she was sitting stressed until she had seen her relax with her dad's arrival.

Kate figured there was no time like the present to go over and introduce herself, although she had to admit she was a little intimidated. She had seen him in the shop working, and while she hadn't been spying on him, she felt like the glimpse made her seem like she'd done something a little bit underhanded.

"Hello. I'm Kate Woolbert. I'll be the new counselor after the holiday break."

She held out her hand as the man stood. His eyes were kind, although maybe a little careworn. His face was tan, and there were several days' worth of beard growth. Just enough to make him look like a reformed bad boy.

Kate shoved the idea aside. She certainly wasn't going to think about the father of her potential student that way.

"I'm Jack Henderson," he said, grasping her hand in a strong, firm grip. But it wasn't so tight as to hurt. She'd shaken hands with her students' parents and felt like she needed to soak her hand in some kind of relaxing warm water afterwards. Jack wasn't like that.

"It's good to meet you, Mr. Henderson. I've been observing your daughter. She seems like a very intelligent and interesting young lady." She smiled down at Lilly, who pressed herself against her father, although there was no fear in her eyes as she looked up. It was like she didn't want to stop touching her dad because she was afraid he might go out of her sight, but she wasn't afraid of Kate.

"Call me Jack, please."

"All right," she said slowly. She typically did call teachers by their surname, but parents were a different case. She preferred that they use her title and last name, so the children didn't get too familiar. It was good to have a professional barrier between them.

"She's quite a young lady," he said, looking down at his daughter with pride.

"Lilly, would you like to come over here and put a sticker on the board? I believe we forgot to do that earlier," Miss Jones said, giving Kate a look that said "If you want to talk to her dad, I'll take her away for you for a few minutes."

Reluctantly, Lilly walked away from her dad, throwing a last look over her shoulder.

"She doesn't like to let you out of her sight," Kate observed, wondering what Mr. Henderson would say about that.

"Ever since her mom died, I'm all she has left. It makes sense to me that she'd want to stick pretty close."

"Do you have trouble getting her to go to school in the morning?"

"Not really." He didn't elaborate.

"Has she spoken at all?" Kate asked, wondering how she could get him to talk about his daughter, or if he even wanted to.

"No. Not a word that I've heard." He drew in a breath and blew it out. "Principal Stevens said that you might be interested in working with her. If you are, I'd definitely be open to it."

"I would love to. She seems like a bright young lady, but... she's been through a really tough time."

"She sure has. She's a lot different at home than she is here at school. If you need to observe her in her... natural habitat," he said with a grin, "you're certainly welcome to come to the candy shop. That's usually where we spend our time after school."

"I saw it when I drove through town the other day," she said, not elaborating on the fact that she had indeed seen it and him as well.

"The shop was in her mother's family. It was her mother's dream to pass it down to Lilly and have Lilly be a candy maker."

"How does Lilly feel about that?"

"I don't know; she doesn't really talk about it." He grinned, not making a joke of his daughter's muteness, but showing by his smile that he had accepted it and knew there wasn't a lot he could do to change it.

"Interesting. If you don't mind, I'd definitely like to take you up on that. I would love to see her with you, and if I'm being honest, I'd love to take a look at the candy shop. The display in the window is absolutely fantastic."

"Lilly helped me with it, but... I learned a lot from Lauren before she died. It's not nearly like what she could do, but not too bad for a man who thought he was going to be a farmer but turned into a candy maker by accident."

Interesting. It didn't sound like Lilly's dad necessarily wanted to be a candy maker. Was he only keeping the shop open for Lilly? Or because of the memory of his late wife?

"I don't officially start as school counselor until after the break, but... I could come by the shop anytime."

"Absolutely. Today is fine. This is our busy time of year, and I'll be there early in the morning and late at night. Stop by anytime."

"All right, I will," she said, and then watched as Lilly finished up quickly with Miss Jones and hurried back to her dad, again pressing herself against his side.

"Interesting."

A child came up then and Jack and his daughter walked away. It was just as well. Kate had a lot to think about.

Chapter Six

Kate adjusted her purse over her shoulder and closed her car door carefully.

She glanced up at the sign above the sidewalk: "Mistletoe Meadows Candy Canes."

Maybe a little creatively uninspired, but descriptive.

Had she heard somewhere that it had been in his family for five generations?

Not his family—hers. His late wife's. Jack's late wife.

No wonder he was working so hard to keep it for Lilly.

At the thought of Lilly, her heart clenched a bit. She really wanted to help the child. How difficult it must be to lose one's mother. Of course, at least she had a caring and loving father who wanted the very best for her.

Thoughts of Kate's own cold childhood tried to push into her mind, but she shoved them aside. That was part of the reason she became a counselor, because she had so longed for a gentle touch, a warm hug, a caring smile from her parents, but they never seemed to have time.

They had taken care of her, that was for sure. Provided her with everything a child could want, except love and attention. They'd been too busy working to pay for all the things they had given her, and anytime she tried to talk to them about it, especially as she got older, they gave her a guilt trip for not being grateful for what they had provided and always wanting more. She hadn't wanted more; she had just wanted... the human connection. The love a child deserves from their parents.

But her parents had done the best they could, and looking back, Kate could hardly fault them. They thought they were providing for her in the very best way possible. And they truly did think she wasn't being grateful when she asked for something different.

Regardless, it had shaped her entire life and landed her here, at Mistletoe Meadows Candy Canes and Jack Henderson's doorstep.

It was a shop, so she didn't have to knock before she pulled the door open and stepped inside.

It was like stepping back in time into an old-fashioned movie, only the smell was minty and somehow old, yet not musty or dirty.

She breathed in deeply, the sugary, sweet candy scent seeming to fill up her soul, like the hug that she'd longed for as a child.

The old-fashioned display in the window, with the mechanical toys that made little clicking and buzzing noises as they moved along, made her smile as she walked along the hardwood floor. They were small, narrow planks, and she guessed the floor hadn't been replaced since the building had been built in the early 1900s.

It probably wasn't on the national historic register, but a part of her felt it should be. She supposed it provided tons of beautiful memories to all the kids who had grown up over the years in Mistletoe Meadows.

How many kids had stood in front of the penny candy display, clutching a nickel or a dime and trying to decide which candy they would choose?

She smiled at the thought.

And somehow the thought made her long for a child of her own to hold her hand and stand and make decisions about what she really wanted. Of course, as a child, her parents probably would have encouraged her to save her money and not spend it frivolously on candy.

"Hey there," Jack spoke, startling her.

"My goodness, I didn't see you back there." He stood behind the mixer, which was silent and still.

"I need to get these candy canes shaped before they cool too much to work with."

"That looks so interesting. Would it be too much to ask for me to be able to watch you?"

"I think that's why we have the store part open to the kitchen. So that people can come in and watch." He looked up with a welcoming smile. "Of course you're welcome to come over and take a look."

Movement caught her gaze, and she realized Lilly stood directly beside her dad, her hands on the counter, shaping candy canes.

"Lilly. I didn't see you there. Looks like you're helping your dad."

Lilly's eyes, bright and shining, looked up as she nodded happily.

The little girl had been well-behaved in school, but obviously here in the shop her entire body seemed to come alive.

"Lilly loves to help."

"I bet she's a great helper." Lilly beamed. Kate's gaze went to the pot on the burner. "So you cook the... it's not called batter?"

"No. We refer to it as syrup. We cook the candy syrup to a specific temperature, and then we put it in strips on a tray to let it cool. Then, before it's completely cold, you have to form those strips into the shape that you want. Obviously, because of the name of the shop, we make a lot of candy canes, but we do have different kinds of candy too."

"You do?" Kate asked, looking around the shelves. There were blue candy canes and green ones, the traditional red and white stripes, as well as solid red and solid white. She could read the different tags with the different flavors underneath. A banana candy cane caught her eye.

"Yeah. I don't make a whole lot of chocolate, but it's probably my favorite thing."

"Your favorite thing to eat, or your favorite thing to make?"

Jack exchanged an amused smile with Lilly. "Both," he said, his brows raised, and he looked at Lilly rather than Kate as he spoke.

The little girl laughed, and a small sound escaped her mouth, but she quickly put her hand over it, stifling her laughter.

Jack didn't seem to notice that his daughter had made a sound, and Kate wondered if that was normal. Perhaps she did often laugh.

"So you two own and run a candy cane shop, and yet your favorite candy is chocolate. Is this something I should report to the candy police?"

Lilly giggled again, her shoulders shaking, but she kept any noise from coming out of her mouth.

Jack looked amused at his daughter, and then at Kate. "We would be guilty as charged. Although, to be fair, both of us love candy canes and eat far more than we should. After all, that's how our store makes a profit."

A little bit of the light dimmed from his eyes after saying that last part, and it made Kate wonder if the reason Jack worked so much was because the store was having financial difficulties.

She remembered what someone had said about Lilly being in the hospital and Jack trying to keep the store afloat for her.

That seemed to insinuate that there might be some trouble. Not to mention, Kate couldn't imagine handcrafted candy canes being a lucrative business.

She glanced again at the displays, noting the prices and trying to figure out how much he would have to sell in order to simply pay rent on the building.

Maybe they owned it outright, and then he'd just have to figure taxes. She hadn't lived in the area long enough to know if taxes were expensive or not. In some places, taxes could break a family trying to make a living.

She'd seen that firsthand in the inner city.

"There. Another tray done. Can you carry this carefully over to the rack?" Jack said, looking at Lilly, who nodded eagerly.

Kate got the impression that Lilly found any job in the candy shop an honor.

As Lilly picked up the tray and turned, she tripped on something and tumbled, barely catching herself before the candies spilled all over the floor.

A micro-expression on Jack's face showed dismay, and then relief settled there as the candy was safe.

Lilly's eyes were big, and her mouth was open, almost as though she was ready to say something, whether it was an apology or an exclamation of surprise or dismay, Kate wasn't sure.

"That was a good catch," Kate said. "You're very light on your feet, Lilly."

Lilly saw the acceptance and compassion on her dad's face, and it seemed to soothe her, because she turned to Kate with a smile that grew wider as she met Kate's gaze.

Carefully, walking very slowly, Lilly carried the tray to the rack that Jack had indicated.

Was it possible that as young as she was, she knew how important the candy shop was to her mother's memory and she was putting too much pressure on her young little shoulders to learn and make her mother proud of her?

She seemed kind of young for that type of issue, but maybe she'd overheard her dad talking to someone about it.

"All right, Lilly. You know what time it is. I'll be up in fifteen minutes, after you've taken your shower, and we'll read a little bit before bed. You do have all of your homework done, right?"

Lilly nodded, and then she put a hand up and wiggled her fingers at Kate.

She didn't give her dad any trouble as she turned toward the back and disappeared into a hallway.

"She loves it down here. She'd spend all day every day here if I let her."

"She's different here than she is at school, that's for sure," Kate said, not wanting Lilly to overhear her.

Jack glanced back toward the hallway and tilted his head to one side as footsteps echoed, showing that Lilly had headed up the stairs, and then a door closed.

"She's a good kid," Jack sighed. "This was her mother's shop, and it was Lauren's dream to have Lilly follow in her footsteps, because it had been in the family for so long. I'm doing everything I can to try to keep it together."

Kate nodded, and she was trying to figure out what kind of questions she could ask that would let her know if the shop was in some kind of financial trouble. Not that it was any of her business and not that she could do anything to help. She might be able to buy a few pieces of candy, but she wasn't going to be able to pay any major bills. She hadn't even managed to find herself a place to live, not one that she could afford anyway. There were some high-end rental places on the outside of town, and a couple of nice houses for sale, but again, they were out of her price range and completely out of her budget.

"I would think this season would be your best sales season," she said, hoping the statement was open-ended enough that if he wanted to talk about his financial issues he could. Perhaps that had something to do with Lilly's issues.

"It's a good thing too. Lilly was sick for a while over the summer, and I'm still paying on the hospital bill. Thankfully, they've allowed me to set up a payment plan, or... the creditors would be after me right now."

"Oh, that's too bad. She looks perfectly healthy."

"She is now. It wasn't anything to do with her muteness. It was just a summer fever that turned into strep throat, and her throat hurt so bad she wasn't drinking anything, so then she was dehydrated on top of it and... they just needed to keep her for a bit."

"And she couldn't tell you, or wouldn't tell you, that there were any issues?"

"No." He sighed again, tidying up the area where they had been rolling out the candy.

"The last school counselor didn't seem to be super interested in her. I'm really hoping that... something changes."

"Well, I'm definitely interested in her, so there's a change."

"Obviously, since you're here after school. You don't have to visit your students outside of the classroom."

"I might not have to, but sometimes that's what a good professional does."

She knew there were teachers who just taught because they got the summers and holidays off. She'd heard them talk about it in college when they were taking the classes. And a person only had to glance at them to know that they felt like their job was confined to the school and the classroom. Some of them didn't even take work home to correct, but only did what they could while in school.

"It's rare to find someone who's so dedicated to their job."

"I don't know if it's dedication to my job, as much as I just care about people, and kids in particular. Lilly is so sweet, and it's so heartbreaking that she lost her mom so early."

"Yeah. I've felt bad for her, having to put up with me as both mom and dad. I don't feel like I do a very good job of either one."

Jack didn't sound like he was fishing for compliments, and he wasn't that kind of person anyway. He was just stating what he felt were obvious facts.

"I don't think any one person would do a good job of being both mom and dad. That's why God gave kids both. Because women are specifically created to be good at the jobs that a mom needs to do, and men are specifically created to be good at dad jobs. And God meant for men and women to pair up and to raise children together."

"I wonder why I ended up raising mine by myself then, you know?" He lifted his shoulder. "If God was so set on moms and dads and about a kid needing a mom and dad, why did my wife die?"

That was a good question, and she didn't blame him for struggling with it.

"I wish I could answer that. I don't have a good answer, other than I don't understand God or His ways, and I'm not supposed to. Isn't that where faith comes in? We just trust when we don't know the answer. And that's how we live by faith."

He huffed out a breath, a short laugh, maybe. "Yeah. That's kind of the conclusion I came to too. God didn't want man to fall into sin, but now that we live in a sinful world, things aren't perfect. Nor should we expect them to be, and it's our own fault. Beyond that, I just have to trust and have faith that God will work things out. That's what the Bible means when we walk by faith and not by sight. I want to see, though. I want to see the why, the purpose behind everything, so then I can know for sure that this is what I'm supposed to do."

"And then it wouldn't be faith, would it?" Kate said, thinking about what he had said and agreeing with him. When the way wasn't clear ahead, or the reasons why weren't given to them, it was just a matter of having faith. And it seemed so simple, so easy, but it's where a lot of people stumbled. Because they couldn't just trust God and His inherent goodness. They saw something bad happening and their faith wasn't strong enough for them to keep walking anyway. So they quit and turned away.

"Life isn't all bad," Jack seemed to be shifting the topic, and Kate appreciated it. While their former line of conversation wasn't exactly depressing, it could be, if she thought about all the people in her life that were no longer living for the Lord.

"It's not. It's mostly good," Kate said, nodding emphatically as though that would make it so.

"I think a lot of it is how we think about it. After all, a situation that looks bad in my eyes could be good to someone else. It's about how we frame it."

"That goes along with the Bible verse that says to focus on things that are right and true and good."

"It kind of does, because there's always some kind of good in a situation, but it's up to us to choose to look at it that way."

"I read a Christian writer at one point, and I remember him saying that when we're saved, God does the sanctification, but our part is the thousands or tens of thousands of small moral choices we make every day."

Jack nodded, setting the bowl in the sink and turning the faucet on to wash his hands. "I think that's true. And those choices begin with the decision of how we're going to allow ourselves to think."

"What you think is what you are," she said a little lightly, because for some reason with Jack, their conversation had gotten serious right away, and she hadn't intended for that to happen. Although, she didn't mind. In fact, she enjoyed finding someone with whom she could share ideas and thoughts and things that she hadn't quite figured out on her own.

"You've got quite a lot of ideas for a candy maker, not that candy makers can't be deep thinkers," she said, afraid she might have upset him.

He laughed instead. "I probably have a lot of things going on in my head that candy makers don't normally."

"Like?" she prompted. She wasn't sure why she was so curious, but she didn't stop to examine it.

He shrugged his shoulder. "A lot of the things that I want are things I can't have, and I'm better off if I don't focus on them."

"I see," she said, more curious than ever. His answer didn't answer anything.

The bell jingled above the door as a cool rush of air floated in, along with a ruggedly handsome man with a thick beard and shining eyes that could possibly contain humor, although they looked somber and serious tonight.

From his uniform, Kate assumed he was the sheriff.

"Everything looking good tonight, Jack?" the man said, his voice businesslike but also concerned. If Kate had to guess, she would say that Jack and the man were friends.

"Looking good, Ben. Appreciate you stopping in."

A shadow of a smile crossed Ben's face. "It's my job." He nodded to Kate and said, "Ma'am."

That was it, and then he turned and walked out the door.

"He's a good sheriff. I never saw hide nor hair of the last guy, but Ben stops in every single night, unless he's out on a call somewhere, and even then, I've seen him walking the streets long after his shift should have been over."

"Quite admirable. Someone who's dedicated to their job."

"Not unlike you." Jack's voice might have held admiration, or perhaps a compliment.

"I don't know that I'm doing a job, so much as I truly feel drawn to Lilly. I can relate to her."

"You've been mute before?" Jack asked, as he finished drying his hands and hung the towel back on the rack.

"No. Of course not."

"I don't know that I would say 'of course.' If Lilly grows out of this, there'll be a lot of people in her life that didn't know that she had several years of never saying anything."

"I suppose you're probably right. But no. She just... there's a lot of potential in her, and..." Kate took a breath. How much of her family history did she want to get into? She wasn't sure if she wanted to get into any of it, honestly, although there was something about Jack that made her want to share.

"I never lost my mother. She's still alive. But I guess I just felt alone a lot of times, because she wasn't very affectionate. And while she was interested and a good mother, for the most part, she just didn't have any emotional connection to me."

"I see. That must have been hard, especially because anyone who looked at you might have thought, 'Oh, she's got a great home life, she's lucky.'"

"Exactly. How could I complain? I couldn't. So I just kind of kept it to myself. But it hurt."

"That makes sense to me. I know that everyone's trial is hard for them, even if someone else might look at it and think, 'Oh, that I could handle that easily.' Probably that's why God didn't give you that trial."

She laughed. "Right? He already knows what we can handle easily, and He gives us something else, because we're not supposed to just have a life of ease and happiness. We're supposed to be growing and becoming more like Jesus. And how else are we going to do that if we don't go through hard things?"

"Yeah. I would agree with that wholeheartedly. Even though the hard things are usually not fun. And sometimes it seems like they're never-ending."

She wondered what felt like it was never-ending to him. The grief from losing his wife? She wanted to ask about her, if they had been high school sweethearts, and if she was his soulmate, and he would never get married again.

But why did she care? She shouldn't. Not about that.

So she kept her mouth shut and didn't say anything.

Not about that. Maybe someday they'd be close enough friends that she could ask.

"I better get upstairs to Lilly. She can take a bath by herself, but I still put her to bed. I know someday she'll not want me to anymore, and I try to always make time for that. Every night."

"I think that's really good. I wish all parents were that conscientious and tried to make time for their children."

She heard the note of sadness in her voice, and it bordered on self-pity. She didn't want that. She wouldn't allow that. Everything that she had gone through had shaped her into the person that she was. If her parents had been perfect, she would have missed the opportunities to grow, and... she wouldn't have become better. At least, that's the way it felt to her.

"Thanks for chatting with me. I enjoyed it," she said honestly. She felt like maybe she had found a friend in this town.

Jack nodded his head. "Stop by anytime. I'm in one of the few professions where I can talk and work at the same time and be just as productive."

She laughed, then put a hand up as she turned toward the door.

She was still deep in thought about the things that they had talked about, and mulling over in her mind how easy her relationship with Jack seemed to be, and almost ran into a lady on the sidewalk.

"Excuse me," she said immediately, sidestepping neatly. At the same time, she realized that the lady must have been just as deep in thought, since she seemed equally surprised.

"Kate. You're out late," Marjorie McBride said, her eyes kind and crinkled, smiling at Kate in the narrow beam of light given off by the street light.

"I am. I was just talking to Jack about Lilly, mostly." She couldn't really say she had to add the "mostly" on, because it wouldn't have been honest to say that that was all they were doing.

"Oh, I'm so glad. The last guidance counselor was a nice lady, but... Lilly could use a little extra attention."

"And I intend to give her everything I can," Kate said, knowing that she'd already promised herself that in her heart. With every student she came in contact with, not just the one she was drawn to. "It may be a little extra, because Lilly seems special."

"I'm glad you see that. I think she is," Marjorie said, smiling fondly.

Lilly wasn't one of Marjorie's grandchildren, but that didn't seem to matter. Marjorie seemed to think just as fondly about her. If she'd ever met a nicer woman than Marjorie McBride, she couldn't remember. And Marjorie had been through a lot of hard times, losing her husband being just one of many. A recent diabetes diagnosis was another, according to Nelly.

"We've kind of taken Jack under our wing and try to include him in the family get-togethers. He's had a hard time of it." Marjorie smiled, but it was a tired smile. And Kate thought about her recent diabetes diagnosis. Was that all that was wrong with her? She thought Nelly had said that Marjorie mostly had that under control.

"He's very good at making candy, but it's not where his heart is."

Kate wanted to ask about that. Where was his heart?

But Marjorie held up a bag. "I needed to stop in at Olivia's shop and grab a couple of her handcrafted candles that she made for a friend of mine. I can get the box together and ship that off in the mail tomorrow. It's nice to check things off my list."

"This time of year, sometimes it's a long list," Kate said, wondering how Marjorie had time to think of friends, with all the family she had around. The woman was practically a saint.

"I don't think I've even started my Christmas shopping. I'm... probably scaling down a bit this year."

Because of finances. Not that she ever went totally crazy at Christmas time, but she did enjoy giving gifts. Still, trying to find a house and moving and dealing with the lease from her last job had definitely put her in a different position this year.

"There's always ways to help. It doesn't necessarily have to be expensive. I like supporting the small shops along our main street," Marjorie lifted a hand and indicated the shops around them, which were all soon closing. "This would be so dark and empty without them."

"I guess that's part of what living in a small town is. You support each other." That hadn't been the way it was in the city. She'd felt isolated and alone, even though she was far from either.

"But you have to nurture it. It's not something that just happens without a lot of work from everyone involved. But that's life, isn't it?" Marjorie said, with an almost inaudible sigh. "I'd better get going. It's past my bedtime."

Kate nodded. "Mine too." They started to walk away, and then Kate stopped. "Oh! If you hear of anyone renting out an apartment, not too expensive, please let me know."

"Absolutely. It didn't even occur to me that you might be looking. I will check a few sources and get back to you."

Of course she would. Marjorie would leave no stone unturned now that she knew. Kate didn't know why she hadn't asked her earlier, although a part of her felt guilty for putting more on the woman's shoulders, since she already seemed so tired.

"Thank you. And... Marjorie?"

"Yes?"

"Take care of yourself, okay? What you said about small towns is true. But there are just some people in a small town that make it what it is, and I have a feeling that you're one of those people."

Marjorie smiled, but it wasn't a triumphant smile. Instead, it was a kind, benevolent smile. "I have a feeling that you're one of those people too."

Marjorie turned and walked away, and didn't notice that Kate stood staring at her, her mouth open. Was she one of those people? She looked around and saw other people doing so much; she didn't really think about how she might look to others. But that was the reputation she wanted to have. One of kind consideration toward others, a positive attitude—not necessarily solving others' problems, and like she and Jack had been talking about, a way of looking at the world that saw the good in every situation, even if it seemed like a bad thing. Like being unable to find a house for rent that she could afford, and having to scale down Christmas.

Maybe, as Marjorie said, there were other things she could do.

Chapter Seven

"Remember last year when we didn't even know who the other was?" Nelly said as she and Roland walked through the back streets of Mistletoe Meadows after midnight, holding hands and enjoying the feeling of having accomplished something worthwhile, since they had just delivered five Christmas trees to houses that didn't have them.

"I know. And I had this irritating person in my real life who considered me her enemy for years, and I had this really compelling person that I met with at night and couldn't stop thinking about."

"Irritating?"

"You can't say that you didn't think the same about me. Worse even." There was laughter in his tone, and Nelly grinned to herself.

"You're right. You're absolutely right, as you usually are."

"Oh, I am? Can I get that recorded?"

"No. Absolutely not. And if anyone asks if I said it, I'll deny, deny, deny."

They laughed together.

"What are you thinking about Kate?" Nelly finally asked. Her friend seemed to be settling down in town okay, although she'd only been there a few days.

"I think she's going to be great. We can definitely use her. But I'm not sure about handing things off to her. Plus, do we really want to give it up?"

"Do you think we can do it with a family?"

They had been trying to start a family for a couple of months, and Nelly had a feeling that she was going to have some good news for Roland at Christmas.

"I don't particularly want to try to shuffle kids and sitters and make our lives even more difficult. Who would? But I can't deny that I love doing it, and I think you do too."

"I do. But you're right. It might be time to pass the torch. Although these will always be some of my fondest memories."

"Not too many people can say they wooed each other and didn't even know who the other one was."

They smiled, their fingers twined together and swinging freely between them, their steps slow and leisurely.

"With children, we probably can't be up late, walking around like this, because they're going to expect us to get up at the crack of dawn and be happy and cheerful."

"Well, I don't expect you to get up at the crack of dawn, but I do expect you to be happy and cheerful. You know how miserable it would be to be married to someone who wasn't?" Roland shivered as though talking about something truly terrible.

Although it would be terrible to be married to someone who couldn't greet the other with a smile and a kind word, who was miserable and complained all the time.

"Have I thanked you lately for being a generally positive, upbeat, kind person? And for being that way with me?" Nelly asked, lifting their joined hands together and placing a kiss on his knuckles.

Instead of allowing their hands to drop, he pulled them to his lips and kissed her knuckles as well. "I think you might have done that this morning, actually, but I don't mind hearing it again. And

I'm pretty sure I told you that I felt like I was the most blessed man in the world, because being married to you these few months have been better than all of the months I spent single."

She tilted her head up and grinned at him.

"I suppose we can get all mushy now, or we could talk about whether or not Kate is the person we want to pass the torch to."

"I honestly don't know that we want to pass the torch to her completely, although she would be really great to add to our list of informants."

Nelly nodded. A lot of their informants had no idea they were informants, but Kate, with her position in the school, would have access to information that not too many people would. There would be some of it that she couldn't share, because of confidentiality laws, but there would be others that were observable and completely reportable.

"Has she found a place to stay yet?" Roland asked as they made it to his truck, and he opened her door for her. She appreciated the small gesture of courtesy. Even though she was perfectly capable of opening her own door, it was just the idea that he was showing deference to her, and a kindness that she appreciated.

"Thank you," she said as she got in. And then she said, "I don't think so."

He jerked his head as he closed her door and walked around his truck.

As he got in, he said, "Isn't there a small efficiency apartment above the candle shop?"

"I think so, but it has nothing. Like, literally it doesn't even have a stove."

"She might not be too picky at this point. She needs a place to stay. As long as she can sleep and have decent meals, I don't think she'd complain. But... maybe she's more high-maintenance than I know."

"No. She's very down-to-earth. And I don't think she'd mind staying there, although I don't think she'd want it to be her permanent residence. She just took that job in the inner city that didn't pay much, and I know she doesn't have a whole lot of savings."

"Sometimes I wonder why jobs that contribute nothing to society pay so much—for example, the owner of a professional football team, or a CEO of a large company. And yet, the very foundation of our society depends on laborers and teachers as well, and yet they don't make much in the way of financial benefits."

"And an inner city teacher would have such a difficult job." Nelly couldn't answer his question, and she knew it was rhetorical. It did seem like pay grades were backwards, and the less a person contributed to society in some meaningful way, the more money they seemed to make.

"So then Kate can give us information, but she might not be a good fit for the actual secret saint?" Nelly said as they drove slowly home. She didn't want to reach out to her friend if Roland didn't think that it was a good idea.

"Tell you what. Let's keep an eye on her and see how she does. She doesn't have to know that it came from us, or that we're thinking about adding her to our network."

"Good idea. A trial run, so to speak."

"Exactly."

Chapter Eight

*J*ack put the last candy cane in the box and then carefully closed it, wrapping the paper neatly and making it look as nice and pretty as he could. This was where Lauren had really shone. She had a flair for making things look pretty. A little bit like herself. Pretty on the outside. Sometimes on the inside, she wasn't always beautiful.

He shook those thoughts aside. She was well-liked in the community, and she did the best she could. He didn't hate her and didn't regret marrying her, although he did regret her dying.

He didn't know why his thoughts were so morbid today, although maybe it had something to do with the announcement that he'd heard on the news that morning. Big Bolts, the chain store that was in pretty much every town over a certain population across the United States, had announced that they were going to put in a candy section, and reading between the lines, he figured the candy would all come from an Asian country that paid their workers peanuts and could afford to ship things across the ocean for less than he could make them in his store and sell them off the shelf.

He couldn't imagine the conditions those workers must be in for that to be profitable for Big Bolts. And Big Bolts was the chain store that had been looking to put a store in just outside of Mistletoe Meadows.

If that happened, it was almost certainly going to take business away from his store. There was no way that some of the people who purchased candy canes from him wouldn't go to the close and convenient and now also carrying candy, Big Bolts.

His phone rang as he put the final touches on the box. It wasn't anything to write home about, but it did look cute if he had to say so himself. Maybe he was getting better at it. It wasn't what he wanted to do, it wasn't where his heart was, but he would do what he had to do in order to keep the inheritance that his daughter deserved alive. Although he might not be able to keep from losing the store.

Sighing, he pulled his phone out of his pocket, saw that it was Noah Parker, who owned the music shop next door, and answered.

"Hey, Noah. What's up?"

"Jack. Glad I caught you. There's an emergency town business meeting tonight, and I was hoping you'd be able to attend."

He looked over at Lilly, who had been shaping warm candy ropes into perfect candy cane shapes, but who had stopped to look up and listen to his phone call. Her brows were puckered together, as though she was worried.

He gave her a reassuring smile before he turned slightly away from her and spoke into his phone.

"Lilly's here. I can't leave her."

"Well, if you could make it, I would appreciate it. We've got some serious business to talk about."

It didn't sound good. He bet it was about Big Bolts. He wasn't the only one who was going to be affected by them putting in a store nearby.

Whatever it was, if it affected Mistletoe Meadows, it affected his bottom line, but even more so, it affected his friends, the people who had been like family to him after his wife had died and left him with a four-year-old little girl. The sweetest girl in the world, and one he loved with a love that actually hurt. He hadn't realized there could be a love like that, not until he had children.

"I'll see what I can do."

"All right. I'll look for you."

He hung up the phone and tried to think. For some reason, Kate came into his mind immediately. He could be wrong, but he was pretty sure he could give her a call, if he had her number, and she would come immediately. But she was a professional. A counselor, working for the school. She wasn't his friend, or a babysitter for him, as much as the line seemed to be blurred somehow in his mind. He had enjoyed his conversation with her and realized that he didn't typically talk to people the way he had with her, opening up about things and discussing stuff that maybe didn't make a huge difference in the scheme of life, but that he enjoyed thinking about. She apparently did too.

No, he wasn't going to call her. Even if he could.

But Mrs. Abernathy might be willing to come over and put Lilly to bed.

He looked up at his daughter, who had moved silently from where she had been working over to his side.

Her hands were sticky; she hadn't even washed them, as she looked up at him, serious and sober and slightly afraid.

He didn't like his little girl being scared.

He put a hand on her shoulder and drew her to him, hugging her tightly and not caring that her sticky fingers were touching him as she hugged him back. Sticky fingers were a normal thing to a candy maker anyway.

"Do you mind if Mrs. Abernathy comes to put you to bed?" he asked gently, looking down at her as she pulled back and looked up at him.

"I know you love her, and she thinks you're just the best thing since sliced bread."

That got a little bit of a smile out of his daughter, and she nodded, although he knew she would rather not. He thought she looked forward to their time together in the evening as much as he did. They were in the middle of reading a good book, and they usually prayed together as well as talked about their day. At least he talked, and she listened. It was the best he could hope for, and honestly, he appreciated the help of all of the experts, but he wondered if his daughter would ever talk again. Something told him that she probably wouldn't.

Regardless, she had nodded, so he pulled his phone out and dialed his neighbor.

$\mathcal{K}$ate shoved her hands deeper into her pockets and hunched down in her coat. A cold front had moved in overnight, and while it hadn't brought any precipitation with it, it had definitely brought lower temperatures. It made it feel like Christmas.

The twinkling lights of the town, the Christmas displays in the windows, and now the weather combined to make Mistletoe Meadows truly feel like a Christmas town from a storybook.

Kate smiled at the cozy feeling.

School had gone well today. She had been enjoying not having a whole lot of pressure on her as she followed the principal's suggestions and visited every classroom. Today she'd spent the entire day with the fifth graders and met some of the McBride children—Marjorie's grandchildren. They were impish boys, growing up into teenagers, but also sweet and kind.

There were some other kids she had her eyes on as well, and while she would have preferred to be making money this month, she was grateful that she could spend the time learning about the children she was going to be helping come the new year.

She looked up and realized her feet had stopped in front of the candy cane shop.

Could she go in again? Jack had been on her mind since she left his store the night before. She didn't particularly want him to think that she was stalking him or anything of the sort, but she couldn't help feeling that there were things that she could do to help Lilly. Plus, she had enjoyed Jack's conversation.

It wouldn't hurt to pop in the way Ben, the sheriff, had popped in the night before.

She wasn't going to stay long.

As she turned toward the door, she almost bumped into an elderly lady who used a cane and leaned a good bit of her weight on it as she reached out to open the candy cane shop door.

"Excuse me," Kate said, reaching for the door to open it for the lady.

"No, excuse me. I've gotten a little unsteady on my feet in my old age. Of course, that's not the only thing that happens in old age." The lady smiled, showing that she wasn't exceptionally upset about old age, just making conversation.

"I know the older I get, the more I realize that I did not appreciate my youth while I had it."

"Oh goodness, girl, you still have youth." The lady, instead of reaching for the door, held out her hand. "I'm Mrs. Abernathy. I'm headed here to help watch Lilly because Jack's going to an emergency town business meeting."

"I'm Kate, the new school counselor, although I don't start until the new year."

"I've heard about you," Mrs. Abernathy said as Kate opened the door and she slowly walked in.

There was an emergency town meeting? Kate didn't have any business in the town, so it made sense that she wouldn't have heard about it, but still, she had wanted to get involved. And she could have watched Lilly, although it seemed like Mrs. Abernathy knew her way around, so Kate guessed that she probably watched her a good bit.

"It's a double blessing," Jack said as Mrs. Abernathy walked in, followed by Kate.

Mrs. Abernathy waved her hand in an "aw shucks" kind of way while Kate grinned. She wouldn't have called Jack a flirt, or even a charmer, but he did seem rather charming as he moved from around the counter where he was stacking boxes to help Mrs. Abernathy take her coat off.

"I appreciate you being able to watch Lilly on such short notice," he said to Mrs. Abernathy, and then he glanced at Kate. "Are you planning on going to the town business meeting?"

"I didn't know about it until a couple of seconds ago," Kate said. And then she remembered her vow to get involved in the town as much as she could. "But I'd love to go if anyone's invited."

"Anyone can go who wants to," Jack said. "I have a vested interest in things, but honestly, all the citizens do, if you shop in any of the town businesses. So it's not just business owners who have a monopoly on stuff."

"Then I'd love to go. But I have no idea where it is or when it is, although I assume it's soon since you already have your babysitter here."

"Yes, it starts in just a couple of minutes, and we're going to be a little bit late."

"I'm sorry. I got here as soon as I could," Mrs. Abernathy said. "That porch is so wobbly that I was afraid to go down it, but I needed to get my umbrella, so it took me a little while to fish it off the porch."

"I'm sorry. If I were more handy, I would give you a hand fixing it, but construction is not really my thing."

"But you make the best candy canes in town," Mrs. Abernathy said with a wink.

"Well, thank you," Jack said, with an amused grin at Kate, who grinned back at him. His were the only candy canes in town, although there was something about his grin that maybe didn't quite reach his eyes.

"You also are a pretty good farmer, too, from what I hear," Mrs. Abernathy said.

"We never did get you out to the farm this summer. I've been too busy. But maybe next year."

"You should hire some help, so you have time to do what you love, as well as what you have to do."

Interesting. Mrs. Abernathy was almost insinuating that Jack had to do the candy cane shop, which Kate had surmised, but it almost seemed like farming was what he really was interested in.

Kate would like to have asked more, but she kept her mouth closed. It really wasn't any of her business, although she wanted to make it hers.

"Lilly was doing her chores in the back. I've already said goodbye to her and was just waiting for you to show up."

"All right. That sounds good."

"I shouldn't be late. I'm not sure what the meeting is about, but it shouldn't be regularly scheduled business, and I would expect it to be over rather quickly."

"All right. Take your time. Lilly and I are friends from way back, and we can occupy ourselves. Same rules?"

"Yes. Her homework is finished, and she's allowed a half an hour of TV. Only shows that are on the approved list, which is hanging on the refrigerator."

"All right. Although the last time we were here, Lilly and I got so engrossed in a book that we never did watch any TV."

"I like that. Thank you for going above and beyond," Jack said.

Kate had to admit she was impressed. A parent who actually put restrictions on their child? It was almost unheard of. So many kids were allowed to do whatever they wanted to. But he obviously put her homework first, made sure she had a limit on her electronics, and preferred books over everything. Plus, he had someone as wonderful as Mrs. Abernathy helping him.

It was too bad she couldn't help Mrs. Abernathy in return. It sounded like she could use it with her porch, but... she wasn't a handyman either.

Although she had met Richard Smoker, who had a place to rent but had just rented it out an hour or two before she showed up. He was a contractor and had mentioned that he donated a certain amount of hours of his time every year around the Christmas season to people who couldn't afford his services otherwise.

She made a mental note to talk to him as soon as she could. Maybe he could help Mrs. Abernathy out.

The idea pleased her, and she found herself smiling as Jack finished putting his coat on and then held the door open for her.

"Thank you," she murmured as she stepped out first.

"The meeting is at the church. I guess I should have said that in case you wanted to go by yourself," Jack said as he shoved his hands in his pockets and braced himself against the wind, similar to her position.

"Oh, I wouldn't have left without you, knowing that you were going in the same direction. Unless you didn't want to arrive with me?" She looked up at him. It hadn't occurred to her that there might be any problem with them walking together, but she didn't want to make assumptions that weren't accurate.

"No problem at all. I'm honored to be able to go with you. In fact, it's much nicer to go with someone than by myself."

"I don't know. Some people like to be alone."

"I spend enough time alone."

Jack didn't say anything more, but it reminded her that he had lost his wife, and he truly didn't have anyone to share his life with, other than Lilly, who was in school all day.

Chapter Ten

*J*ack opened the church door for Kate and held it while she walked through. The warmth pouring out was welcome, and he could see her relax as she walked in. It always took a little while after the first cold weather of the season to acclimate to the weather before it stopped bothering him.

It was a good thing, getting acclimated, allowing oneself to be cold. He'd read the latest research and knew that the uncomfortableness was good for his body. That didn't make it any easier.

The entire way from his candy shop to the church, he'd been thinking about Kate. She just seemed to fit beside him. Better than anyone ever had, and he felt comfortable with her. She was a good friend. And obviously she cared about Lilly. He appreciated that probably more than anything, since he felt totally inadequate to be raising her by himself and appreciated any help he could get.

"Thank you," Kate murmured as he walked in behind her, allowing the door to close and keep the rest of the cold air out.

He lifted his hand as they walked in, and Noah Parker, the music shop owner two doors down from the candy shop, smiled from the podium.

"Hey, Jack. We've been waiting on you."

"You didn't have to hold the meeting up for me," he said, surprised, but pleased that they did. He supposed he shouldn't have been surprised; it was a small town and they looked out for each other.

He could see the McBride family sitting to the left, and he moved in that direction.

"Do you want to sit over here with me?" he asked Kate, who seemed to be standing uncertainly. He felt a little bit bad because he'd kind of dragged her along with him. Maybe she hadn't really wanted to go.

Relief moved over her face.

"If you don't mind, yes? I know a few people in town, but I feel a little bit out of my element here."

"Everyone's pretty relaxed. Obviously, since they held the meeting up for us."

"You, not me," she said with a smile.

"If they knew you were coming, they would have waited on you too. You show up to two meetings in a row, and everyone will assume you're a lifelong member."

He moved a chair and held it for her while she sat down, and then he sat down beside her, nodding at Judd and Jones, who had married two of the McBride girls.

"All right, now that Jack is here, we can call the meeting to order." Noah tapped a gavel on the stand. Even though the meeting was always very informal, Noah looked serious and businesslike as he conducted it. It helped set the tone.

"We just got news that Big Bolts has requested approval to put a store in just outside of town, and we already knew the state is in the early stages of planning on making a bypass with an easy on, easy off ramp for Big Bolts and the shopping conglomerate that will probably go with it." Noah lifted a shoulder. "Everything is in the early planning stages, but as a small business owner, this concerns me."

"As well it should. If this happens, the downtown of Mistletoe Meadows will die, like every other small town that's had the big box store go in along with the bypass. It takes all the traffic and routes it around town." Marjorie McBride spoke up, and although she seemed very tired, her words were firm.

"Exactly. We definitely need to fight this. There's no way we can allow this to happen." Jones, married to Amy McBride, nodded at his mother-in-law. "Amy and my veterinary clinic doesn't exactly depend on the traffic going through town, but if our town dies, our business will die as well."

"Same here. As the town doctor, the box store isn't going to affect me, nor the bypass at first, but eventually, as people lose their livelihoods, it will. Also, not to muddy the waters, but I've been so busy in my practice that I'm thinking about hiring a second doctor to help me." Terry, who used to be Terry McBride, sat beside her husband, Judd.

There were murmurs that went through the crowd, probably both about what she had said about the bypass and about her hiring a new doctor.

"Well, that's good news about the second doctor in town. I like to hear about business expanding." Noah spoke from the podium.

Jack figured that, while he was not for the box store nor the bypass, he ought to present the other side. Because there was another side.

When several other people stood up and spoke, but no one spoke in favor of either one of the two happenings—he decided that it was probably his turn to stand up and say what maybe he didn't really want to.

As quiet settled over the meeting, Noah looked around.

"I think we've heard from about everyone. Except you, Jack. I'm sure that you're against both of these things."

Noah said it like it was a given, and it pretty much was, but there was another side.

Jack looked down at Marjorie McBride. He did not want to disagree with her or start an argument or fight with her. The woman was too kind to hold it against him, but he didn't want to be disrespectful either.

Wondering whether he should speak or whether he should just let it go, he glanced at Kate.

"You have something to say. Say it," she whispered to him.

How did she know?

He didn't dwell on that, though, but having got the prompting that he needed, and he slowly stood to his feet. He rubbed the back of his neck and took in a deep breath before he started to speak.

"I agree with everything that's been said here. I don't particularly want a box store to ruin the small town atmosphere of Mistletoe Meadows. I also am personally, completely against the bypass. It will take traffic away from our town, and people who might have gone through and maybe not stopped this time, but come back because of how quaint and cute it is, or maybe someone would have seen an advertisement along the street or whatever. I don't need to go over that with everyone. You're all aware of that."

"You are for it?" Noah asked, sounding surprised.

"I'm not. But there is another side."

"Multimillion-dollar companies making more money off the backs of working people!" someone said from over on the left-hand side of the room. Jack couldn't see exactly who it was, and he didn't recognize the voice.

"That wasn't what I was thinking," Jack said, his words not coming out as firm as he wanted them to. He cleared his throat and tried again.

"Well, then what were you thinking?" Another woman's voice spoke before he could answer.

"Give him some time. The man's trying to find his words," Marjorie McBride said, and although her voice still sounded tired, there was a firmness to it that settled the room right down, and no one dared to speak.

He nodded at Marjorie and gave her a little smile. She tilted her head and seemed to be watching him intently, interested in what he had to say and willing to listen. He looked down at Kate. She looked at him almost exactly the same way. That was enough to enable him to open his mouth.

"I feel like there are some pros to having the box store in town."

"I knew it! You've sided with the millionaires!"

"Billionaires!"

There were murmurings all through the crowd, and Jack wasn't sure where all the voices came from.

He spoke anyway. "I take a lot of pride in my work, and I make a good quality product. But it is very expensive. I can't make money if I don't charge according to the hours that I work and mark it up enough to make a profit—enough for me to live on. That means that sometimes people are priced out of my products, and that's just the way it goes. But that doesn't mean that there aren't people who still want to buy candy canes. Should I keep them from buying candy canes just because they can't buy them at my shop? I don't think so. I guess what I'm saying is, there are people—me included at times—who need to find essentials at the cheapest price possible. And maybe a few things that aren't so essential, like candy and music and candles." He looked at Olivia, who made the handcrafted candles in Mistletoe Meadows. She didn't look overly happy, but she didn't seem upset with him either. "I'm not talking about making the millionaires money. I'm talking about regular folks who maybe don't want fancy candy canes, but just want some inexpensive things to hang on their Christmas tree or to give to their children to eat. They should have a place to buy those things."

"Then they can go to a box store two hours away in Harrisonburg."

"It's two hours. And there's gas for the trip there and back. Is that really what we want to do? Price people out of things just because we are concerned about our own selves? Can we think about others?"

"I guess he has a point. I hadn't really thought about it like that." Marjorie McBride's voice rang through the room, and the silence after she spoke was loud and a little scary.

"That's a good point," Noah echoed. "A box store is not all bad."

"No. It's not. I'm not saying I want it to come in, because obviously that would be competition for what I'm doing and for my friends who have businesses as well. But I don't know that people who would buy handcrafted candy canes are all of a sudden going to go get them at the box store either. It might not be as bad as I think."

"That doesn't solve the problem of the bypass. If they put the bypass in, then that will draw traffic away, and surely you don't have anything good to say about that?" Mrs. Marrey spoke out from the other side of the room.

"Well, actually..."

There was a murmur through the crowd, and Noah banged the gavel a little bit more firmly than he had the last time.

"Let's let him speak," Noah said, a little bit of a warning in his tone.

Ben stood beside the podium, back against the wall, hands folded over his chest, weapon obvious at his side, his uniform giving him the cloak of respectability and deference.

"You're right. If we divert all traffic away from downtown, it will die. There's no question about it. We've seen it all across America. But I have an idea that... as far as I know, has never been tried before."

"What's that idea?" Noah asked, sounding intrigued and not as impatient as Jack might have been afraid. Noah was definitely a man with a head on his shoulders and a very good person to be running a meeting like this.

"I propose that whatever bypass the state puts in only allows trucks to bypass the town. We make the cars go through. That would get rid of some of the heavy traffic, keep our roads a little bit in better repair, and keep the people who are most likely to be stopping at our shops in the town, while we get the people who are less likely to stop —and also more in need of not being stopped in the traffic jams that sometimes ensue as too many cars try to go through the town. In other words, we keep the truckers working while keeping the people in cars coming through our town."

"That is extraordinary. I've never even... would that be possible?" Noah asked, a rhetorical question, because as far as Jack knew, there was no one in the room who could answer that.

"I was also thinking that maybe we could allow certain cars to use the bypass as well. Perhaps locals or in-state residents. I don't know, just a thought."

"I really like the truck idea. I'm not sure about the cars. But we could think about it and see if we can get a state rep to talk to us about it."

Jack had been thinking about it for a while. The rumors of the bypass had been going on for a decade or more, and it had made him sit up and take notice. Every town that put a bypass in, the downtown died. That was just what happened.

But it made sense to take the trucks away, but not the cars. It would be a win-win for everyone. Cars could get through the town without the big backups that sometimes happened, especially in the fall and winter seasons when tourists flocked to Mistletoe Meadows, and trucks would be safer away from town. It would get them on their way faster too, since most drivers were paid by the load or mile, and not by the hour.

He'd never mentioned his idea to anyone before, but it seemed to go over well.

Chapter Eleven

"We definitely have some things to think about now," Noah said, over top of the murmurings, which died down when he started to speak.

"I guess we're kind of shooting ourselves in the foot if we keep the box store from coming in. We'll miss out on the lower prices and shorter drive as well," a voice said from the other side of the room.

"Yes. While some of the practices of the big box stores are not exactly what I would like to see, there's no doubt that they're able to offer products at a less expensive price point. There are people in town who definitely could use that, and it would be a blessing to them. It's foolish for me to prevent that from happening just because of my politics and personal disdain for big companies," the voice came from the other side of the room. It was still in an area that Jack couldn't see very well, but it sounded like someone who had spoken earlier against the idea.

He hadn't meant to talk anyone into anything; he'd only meant to present the other side.

He glanced over, and Kate's eyes were on him. She smiled and leaned closer.

"You did a great job."

"Thanks," he said, and somehow her compliment made him feel warm all the way to his toes.

The meeting had moved on, and they took care of a few different items, but as Jack suspected, it didn't run long.

"And the last thing that we need is someone to volunteer to help Marjorie McBride with the town Christmas festival. Marjorie usually does it all by herself, but we don't want to continue to take advantage of her. Would anyone be willing to help?"

"You should do that," Jack said, glancing at Kate and seeing her biting her lip.

"I was just wondering if I was too new. Do you think people will resent me?"

He glanced around and then lifted his brows. "You don't see anyone else jumping on it."

She took a breath, similar to the one he had taken when he needed extra fortification to stand up and speak his piece.

"I'll help her," Kate said, her voice seeming a little uncertain.

"That's wonderful. I couldn't think of a better person." Noah looked down at the paper in front of him and wrote a name down.

"Does he know you?" Jack asked, knowing that Kate had just moved to town not that long ago.

"Through Nelly. I've met him several times. He's a nice guy."

Was that jealousy that ripped through him, leaving him feeling a little cold and annoyed?

"He's right. You'll be excellent at that."

He had to say something. He couldn't let Noah be the only one giving her a compliment. And he wasn't quite sure why that was.

"All right, I'd like to go back to the first item of business. I have on my paper that I wanted to appoint someone the head of a small business alliance for Mistletoe Meadows. I originally wanted it to be so they could protect the local shops, but maybe just protect the local shops' interests, and while also giving the townspeople the opportunity to have the very best services possible, and making people's commute through Mistletoe Meadows, if it was strictly necessary, as smooth as possible as well. That means you'll be working with local and state authorities and planning commissions as well for the county and the state."

"I think Jack is the obvious man for the job," Roland said, glancing at Jack, who felt a bit of an electric shot go through him. He hadn't come to the meeting thinking he was going to be appointed to anything.

"I was thinking the same thing." Noah nodded.

There were some murmurs, and then several other people spoke up and agreed.

"Will you take the job?" Noah flat out asked Jack.

Jack did not want to, but someone needed to do it.

"We need a shop to feature at the Festival, and I propose that if Jack takes that position, we feature his candy cane shop at the Festival this year." Marjorie McBride spoke clearly. Her words caused a murmur to go through the room, then several people called out an assent.

"I will." Jack knew he needed to answer the call to help his town, and adding the Festival shop feature made it a no-brainer. He hadn't thought about it any farther than that, but he supposed he didn't need to. He was hoping that someone with a cool head, who could see both sides, would be in charge, and... apparently that was him. Did he have a cool head? He thought he could see both sides.

The meeting broke up not long after, and he found himself standing beside Kate, talking to the McBrides.

After a few minutes, they walked away, with the McBride children seeming to want to get their mother home.

"Would you like me to walk you to your car?" Jack asked Kate. There was just something in him that said that since they'd walked there together, he was responsible for getting her home safely, even though he knew that there really wasn't any such thing. She was perfectly capable of getting herself to her car.

"I'd love that."

They spoke to a few more people on their way to the door, where they grabbed their coats and put them on before heading out into the night.

"You did a really great job in there. I was completely against both ideas until you spoke, and then you really made me see that while I still am not super excited about the changes that might happen here, it might be a good thing for the community in general."

"I think so, if we do it in a smart way. I didn't mention it at the time, but some of the tax revenue that's generated by the big box store going in could be used to advertise the downtown. That might mitigate the loss of revenue. I don't know if we can put that directly into any agreements that we make with them or not."

"That's an excellent idea."

"Yeah, I don't know. I suppose we'll see how it pans out. I mean, there will be taxes coming in from that, obviously. So we might as well make good use of them and try to use them to offset any of the negative consequences. I was also thinking that perhaps people who commute through Mistletoe Meadows could somehow have some kind of permit, similar to an EZ Pass, where they're allowed to use the bypass as well, you know?"

"That's a great idea. You should have said that back there." Kate huffed out a breath. "I guess if you're in charge, though, you'll be the one talking, and you can present those ideas to the various people who need to hear them."

"Yeah, I guess I just didn't have everything organized in my head. I wasn't expecting to have to speak on that tonight...I would have been more prepared had I known."

"You did a great job."

"I hope I didn't push you into helping with the Christmas festival if you didn't want to."

"Oh, not at all. I'd planned to get involved in the community. I love that kind of thing, and I thought I would do more of it at my last job, but... it just didn't work out that way. So actually, you did me a favor. Even coming into this meeting, I told myself that I wanted to get involved."

"Well, you're definitely going to be involved. The community Christmas festival is a really big thing."

"I don't know. Maybe people will find out I'm doing it and decide to stay away. Sometimes small towns can kind of circle the wagons against newcomers."

"I can't disagree with you, but I don't think Mistletoe Meadows is like that. Especially since you know the McBrides. That gives you an in that not a lot of people have."

"You would know, having grown up here."

"True. Although I grew up outside of Mistletoe Meadows, on the farm out there."

Kate seemed to hesitate, and then she said, "Are you just in the candy shop because of your late wife?"

Wow. That was a question he wasn't expecting to have to answer today. It wasn't something that he typically talked about with anyone. But he didn't want to ruin the rapport that he'd developed with Kate, and he found himself wanting to answer her anyway.

"It's for my daughter. That's her heritage. So yeah, I would rather be on the farm—that's mine. That's what I love, and it's what I wanted to pass down to my children."

"Lilly is yours too," Kate said.

It was a simple statement, but it hit hard.

"You're doing so much to keep the candy shop alive because it was important to Lauren, but in the process, you're losing what was important to you, if I am not mistaken." She paused for a moment and then she said, "And if I'm not overstepping my bounds, either."

"You're not overstepping. You... said something that I hadn't even dared to think. Or maybe I just hadn't considered it. After all, I guess I assumed that Lilly would want what was her mother's."

"But maybe she wants what was her dad's as well."

"I'll have to think about that," he said. Was he really being blind? Was he doing his daughter a disservice by only giving her one parent's dream?

Maybe she'd have a dream of her own that wouldn't include the candy shop, and he would have spent all that time and struggle trying to keep everything afloat when she didn't really want it after all. But if he lost it and she did want it, he wouldn't be able to get it back.

But the same was true of the farm. It was coming down to him either needing to sell the candy shop or sell the farm, because he wasn't doing a very good job of trying to keep up with both, and he couldn't afford it either.

They walked the rest of the way to Kate's car in silence. The walk had gone quickly. As she stopped beside it, he automatically put a hand on her door handle.

He didn't want the night to be over. He...wanted to spend more time with her.

"Thanks a lot. I think Mistletoe Meadows is pretty safe, but I'm new, and I do appreciate you walking with me."

"It was just a few steps past where I needed to be." He paused, wanting to somehow extend the conversation and his time with her, but not knowing how.

"You don't happen to know of any places for rent, do you?" she said, and it took him a little bit to understand that she was not saying good night. Here he was trying to figure out how to extend their time together, and all he needed to do was pay attention and answer a question.

"No. I'm sorry. I really don't." Even as he said that, he thought of the old farmhouse. There wasn't anyone living in it since Bryan had moved into the new house when their parents sold out and moved to Texas. He supposed he could rent it to her.

"That's too bad. I'm staying in a hotel, and I definitely can't afford it. Funds are running low, and I'm not even going to start my new job until after the holidays." She abruptly stopped and then shook her head and put a hand up. "I'm sorry. That is not your problem. I... just if you see anything or hear of anything—"

"The farmhouse is empty. It's perfectly fine to live in. Lauren wanted to be close to the candy shop when we got married, and I moved out. My brother moved into the new house when my parents moved to Texas, and it's been empty ever since."

"I hate to talk about money, but it would probably depend on how much you're charging as to whether I say yes."

He hadn't considered renting it out and had no idea how much he should charge. And to top it off, he didn't want to charge too much and have Kate turn him down. Somehow, having her there seemed very, very important.

"I could use some help in the candy shop. But I haven't been making enough money to pay for it. I... wouldn't be putting you on payroll or anything."

All of the hassle and extra money that it would take for him to do payroll had discouraged him from even trying. But if they bartered help in the candy shop for rent, it would save him needing to pay her or do the payroll setup.

"I don't know that I could help you that much. I will have my full-time job after the holidays."

"It wouldn't be that much. Honestly, whatever you could do would be wonderful, a huge help."

"Are you sure?" she asked, biting her lip.

He tried not to allow his eyes to dwell there, but met her gaze.

"I'm sure. You could also help some with Lilly if you'd like. We can talk again after you start making money, and when work slows down after the holidays."

"That's fair. Okay. That makes me feel a little better. And I definitely can get some time in now, since I'm just observing, and now I have the community Christmas festival that I'm working on. But beyond that, I'm wide open and I would have some extra hours."

"All right then, it's a deal. I can show it to you tonight if you'd like. I haven't been out there for a month or more, but it's livable."

"Why don't you just give me directions? And if it's truly okay with you, I'll just go stay there."

He wouldn't have to have Mrs. Abernathy stay longer with Lilly, which he would appreciate. Although there was a part of him that didn't want Kate to go out alone, even though it was perfectly safe. "That would work out great. Sounds good."

"Is there a key or something?" she asked.

He laughed. "Don't laugh, but the front key is under the mat. It's not like we get a lot of visitors out there, and there's nothing to steal."

"Oh. Okay. I won't laugh."

Very cliché. He knew it, but that's where they'd always kept it.

"You won't be alone. My brother goes around and checks on it almost daily. He farmed the fields this year, and he's over there for that, too."

"I get it. Okay."

"If you give me your number, I'll text you the address. GPS will take you right to it."

She rattled off her number. He had to admit, it did not make him sad to have it.

"Thank you," she said.

She pursed her lips, as though thinking about something, and then she said, "Would it truly be okay if I worked with Lilly some? I mean, in an unofficial capacity. I don't actually start at the school until after the holidays, but Lilly is special."

"I'm glad you think so," he said, her words bringing a smile to his face. "And yes. Absolutely. She seems to like you a good bit, and if you think there's anything you can do to help..." He allowed his words to trail off. He couldn't deny that his heart skipped a few beats, thinking that someone would be able to help Lilly. He had done everything he could think of, and most of the time when he took her to specialists, they said to just allow her to heal in her own time. But surely there was something he could do to help his daughter through the trauma of losing her mother. It thrilled him to know that there was someone who was willing to help.

"Any time you spend with her can be put toward the rent."

She waved her hand in the air. "Don't worry about it. I... this is what I do. It's what I love."

He sighed an internal sigh of relief. He had been afraid that he wouldn't be able to afford it.

"I can't allow you to do that for free."

"I insist. And you're helping me out of a huge bind. I don't have enough money to continue to stay at a hotel, but I also don't have enough money to come up with a down payment, security deposit, and pay rent on a house or apartment. And there's nothing here anyway. The closest place I've been able to find is an hour and a half away."

"I guess we're even then."

"I haven't done anything yet. I haven't helped you in the shop, and I haven't done anything for Lilly either."

"Just the fact that you're interested makes me happy."

She smiled at him, and they shared a look that seemed a little longer than strictly necessary. He didn't know if she was feeling anything like what he was, but he wanted to reach out, to touch her, to share more than just smiles and looks. To share a physical touch, something that connected them in a tangible way. But instead of reaching out, he fisted his hand and nodded as she said, "I better get going. Thanks again."

"Text me when you get there, and let me know that everything's okay."

"I will. But as long as there's some kind of bed, even if it's just a couch or a blanket on the floor, I'll be happy."

"I want to know if there's heat, running water, and electricity. Okay?" He lifted his brows until she nodded. He could just see her going out there and not even being able to get in and sleeping in her car in the driveway. That seemed like something Kate would do. She didn't seem like a fussy, particular kind of person, but the kind that rolled with things and did her best with whatever was set in front of her. He liked that.

He didn't want to, but he watched her as she drove away and her tail lights faded out of sight down the street. There was something about Kate.

Chapter Twelve

"And who is this?" Kate said, as she pointed to what was obviously a person in Lilly's drawing. Kate had decided to do art therapy, trying to draw Lilly out a little, figure out what was going on in that head of hers.

Lilly looked up at her with sad eyes. Because it looked like there were earrings in the person's ears, Kate guessed that it was a woman.

"Your mother?"

Lilly's eyes widened in surprise, and then she nodded.

"She was very beautiful—that's what gave it away," Kate said, looking again at the picture that Lilly had drawn.

"Would you like to write a sentence about your mother at the bottom?" Kate asked gently, hoping that she could stir a little bit of something else in Lilly, but Lilly shook her head.

"That's fine. You don't have to. The picture is beautiful the way it is. Your mommy was a very special person."

Lilly nodded slowly and looked down at the picture, her mouth twisting a bit, but she still didn't say anything.

Slow, baby steps, Kate reminded herself.

"I think that's enough for today. You did an excellent job, and I'd love to be able to hang this picture up somewhere, unless you would like to hang it on your refrigerator?" Kate asked.

Lilly nodded eagerly.

She reached for the picture. Apparently Lilly wanted to hang it on her own refrigerator.

Kate hid her smile.

"Let's ask your dad and see what he says."

They pushed back away from the makeshift table that they had set up at the side of the candy cane shop, and Lilly grabbed the paper, running over to her dad and waving it.

Jack, looking rather handsome in his white apron and rolled-up sleeves, glanced down at his daughter, saw her animated and excited expression, and his own face brightened in a huge smile as he looked up and his eyes found Kate's, questions in them.

Kate shook her head and then said, "Lilly drew a picture of her mother, and we were hoping it would be okay for her to go up and hang it on your refrigerator?"

"Of course. I should have thought of that before. We have lots of pictures of Mommy on the refrigerator, but none that you drew yourself. You go right ahead and put it wherever you want to." Jack looked with so much love at his daughter that it tugged at Kate's heart. She didn't want the two of them to continue to suffer, and she prayed fervently that she would be able to do something that would break through the wall of silence that Lilly had built around herself.

Once they had talked a bit more and Jack had sent her up to get a shower, he waited until he heard her steps climbing upstairs before Jack looked back at Kate. "That's encouraging." It was a comment that was also phrased as a question.

Kate nodded her head. "I thought so. She almost seemed ready to speak, although when I asked her if she wanted to write a sentence about her mother, she declined."

"I know it has something to do with her mother's death. I don't know if Lauren said something to her, or if she saw something that traumatized her, or if she feels guilty somehow. I wish I knew what the problem was, so that I could help her." Jack ran his hand along the counter, his fingers fisted.

Kate's heart went out to him. Obviously, his daughter was exceptionally important to him, and it warmed Kate's heart to see a parent who cared so much about their child.

"I'll see if I can get to the bottom of it. Maybe we never will. Maybe she doesn't even know. But the fact of the matter is, she can speak, and I think once we knock a hole in that wall, the words will start tumbling out faster than she can stop them. I just don't know what will punch that hole, you know?"

"That's kind of what the doctor said." Jack looked frustrated. "That eventually she'd start talking, because there was nothing physically wrong with her. It's just... it's been years."

Kate nodded. She could understand the frustration. No one wanted to see their child miss essential parts of their childhood because they were unable, or unwilling, or whatever it was, to speak.

Jack looked around, as though he were trying to get his bearings. It was then that Kate realized he seemed a little frazzled.

"Is there something else wrong?" Kate asked.

Jack blew out a breath and then gave a small laugh. "Good problems, I guess. You know that the town nominated my shop to be the featured attraction at the festival opening, which I appreciate, since I just lost one of my biggest customers this year."

"Oh no."

"Yeah. They've been on the fence for a while, and I'd hesitated getting started on the things they normally order because I didn't want to have a huge stock that I couldn't sell, and they order a custom candy cane that doesn't get sold anywhere else."

"And they didn't order it this year?"

"No. They went with a larger company—it's cheaper, offshore, and I just can't compete."

"Oh, that's too bad," Kate said, wishing there was something she could do about it. It made sense that companies wanted to go with a less expensive option. She couldn't fault them for that. The problem was when those things were less expensive because of fewer governmental regulations and taxes and red tape. If they were exploiting their workers, that was a different situation altogether.

She blew out a breath. "So... it's a good thing that you're being featured in the festival, but...?"

"Yeah. So now I have the time and resources to do the festival; I just feel terrible taking time away from Lilly to really do what I would like to do."

"Well, you have a helper now, remember?"

"I didn't even ask how things went at the farmhouse," Jack said, shaking his head as though frustrated at himself.

"You have a lot of things on your mind." Of course he did. His daughter who hadn't spoken, grief over losing his wife, and huge financial responsibilities. Plus, he wasn't even doing what he wanted to do. "Everything was fine. It might have been a little bit dusty, and you could tell that there hadn't been anyone in there for a while, but no animals had made any inroads, and the key was right where you said it would be."

"I'm happy about the animals and the key." He grinned. "Is it going to be suitable?"

"Yes. Absolutely. It's more than I expected and has everything I could possibly need. It's even prettier in the daytime. I came out the door this morning and saw cows grazing in the pasture. I will be sad to leave it."

"Yeah. It's gorgeous there."

Jack didn't say anything else, but it was obvious that he would much rather be living at the farmhouse than in town at the candy shop.

Kate opened her mouth and then closed it again. She wanted to ask him if he really thought it was necessary for him to make the sacrifice to keep the candy shop open, but it wasn't her place to question that. Maybe there was some way that he could close the shop until Lilly was old enough to make a decision about whether or not she wanted to open it. Jack could keep the recipes safe, or maybe even hire someone to run the shop while he farmed.

Again, that wasn't her business. It wasn't her area.

"I don't want to impose upon you. You probably have a lot of other things you want to be doing."

"We agreed that I was going to help you. I can help you in the candy shop; I can help you with Lilly. I can do both. Even once Lilly goes to bed, I can give you a hand in the shop. I will need to go to bed at a decent hour, though, since I've committed to going to school, even though it's in an unofficial capacity."

"Of course. But that would be amazing. If you could help with Lilly and then help in the shop after she goes to bed, I would be so grateful."

"All right then. I'm looking forward to it. Maybe you can share some of your candy-making secrets with me."

He laughed. "There really aren't any secrets. Although I was thinking about doing some historic candy recipes for the Christmas festival. They'll take a little extra time, and that was where my sticking point was."

"Well, hopefully you're unstuck. I will give you a hand, and if it comes right down to it, I could probably even come into the store before school."

"You need to sleep sometime," Jack said.

Kate smiled at the protective tone in his voice, but she could bat that ball right back at him.

"So do you." He looked a little abashed and then he nodded.

"You're right. Although this is the busy time of year, and I expect to be exhausted by the time it's over. But hopefully, it'll be profitable as well."

His tone dropped a bit, as though he didn't expect that to happen this year.

"Is there another supplier that could pick you up?" she asked, having absolutely no knowledge of that business.

"Maybe. But typically I shop around in summer, if I have to. For the last few years, I haven't needed to, because this supplier has taken everything that I was able to make."

"That's too bad."

No wonder the idea of having the big box store come in was adding stress for him. If he was already struggling, if it just took a few customers, that would be a few too many.

"Honestly, though, I have to remind myself that everything happens in God's time. Not just the suppliers and people who buy candy canes, but whether or not my daughter ever talks again, or whether I end up making candy for the rest of my life, when that wasn't what I expected. God is in control, and His timing is perfect." He lifted his shoulder and put a palm up, as though showing that there was nothing he could do.

"I agree. That's a really hard thing to accept. We want to change things; we want to rail against why we're not getting what we want and then try to manipulate things in order for us to get it, and often that backfires."

"Exactly. Though I do believe that we're supposed to work as hard as we can."

"I agree."

"But then we're to leave the rest in God's hands and not fight and kick and do things that we shouldn't in order to get our way."

"Yeah." She thought about her housing situation. Maybe she would have gone after a house she couldn't afford, borrowed money from someone, or even taken a house that was two hours away, knowing that she shouldn't have, but as she waited, God opened up the perfect opportunity. Of course, she hadn't had to wait exceptionally long. Not like Lilly. She'd been mute for years.

"Yeah. It really is hard not to take matters into our own hands and try to do something that we shouldn't."

They stood there for a moment, both of them lost in their thoughts, before Kate glanced around. "Do you want me to start tonight?"

"I was wrapping up. I need to figure out exactly what my

priorities are, but if you show up tomorrow, I will not turn you away."

"All right, sounds good. I will need to attend the regular meetings for the Christmas town festival."

"I know. And I'm excited for you to be in charge of that with Marjorie."

"I guess I would be working with you pretty closely anyway, since you're the featured shop."

"Yeah. It's an honor. And also a great boon for my business."

"I'm happy it happened for you."

"Same. I better get up to Lilly. Thank you again for being a little bit of brightness in my life. I had gotten some bad news with the suppliers and everything today, and you have me hopeful again."

"That makes me feel good. I'll see you tomorrow."

He lifted a hand in acknowledgment before Kate turned and gathered her things up to head back out of the shop. Her heart hummed a merry Christmas tune, and she couldn't keep the smile that turned her lips up off her face. Suddenly, the future looked very, very bright.

Chapter Thirteen

Jack tore the plastic wrap off the roll and placed a candy cane on top of it, carefully folding the edges and bringing them together the way Lauren always had. She had made it look easy, and when he had first started trying to do it, he had ended up with crinkled balls of mess, but eventually, after he'd had to do it, he'd gotten fairly good at it. Sometimes he could even convince himself he enjoyed it.

He glanced over in the corner, where Kate sat with Lilly, earnestly pointing at something on a piece of paper in front of them and talking to Lilly, who nodded her head.

Lauren's old music box sat behind her on a shelf. He'd mentioned when they came in that he had put some things out that Lilly had enjoyed playing with. He hadn't mentioned that he'd put them away for a while because he thought the memories were probably too sad for both of them.

Lauren might not have been the love of his life, but they had spent a lot of time together, and he would be lying if he said he didn't miss her or didn't feel sad to think that she was gone.

But most of his emotions were wrapped up in Lilly and how devastated his daughter was.

Still, he had brought some things out of his bedroom that would work for them to play with in the candy shop, without bringing a whole bunch of Lilly's toys down from upstairs. He tried to keep the candy shop fairly clean and free of clutter. Not to mention it had to be sanitary as well.

He wrapped another candy cane, pulling the bow tight with a flourish and looking up as the bell jingled over a customer's head as someone walked in.

He smiled when he saw Summer McBride strolling in, a cowgirl hat on her head and boots on her feet.

She grinned at him. "Hey there, Jack. How's business?"

"It's going well. This is the best time of year," he said. He lifted his brows. "But I assume you're not in here to buy candy canes?"

"No. I came to talk to Kate. She had said something to one of the children about needing to talk to me, and I decided that instead of sending a message back through school, I would just try to find her in town. I asked at the feed store, and they pointed me here."

"Yeah. She's helping me with Lilly, and then in the shop some as well."

"I heard she's living in the old farmhouse. It's beautiful."

"Yeah. I'm a little jealous. She has a much better view than I do in the morning."

"I don't understand why you don't move back out there. You love it so much," Summer said, shaking her head.

He didn't have an answer for that. Why hadn't he moved back out? Lauren had wanted to move to the candy shop when they got married, and that just made sense, since that's where she worked every morning. And when there wasn't anything to do on the farm, he helped her as well. Eventually, the candy shop had taken over, and he left his brother with more and more work to do on his own.

"I'm sure they will be happy to see you," he said. Summer nodded and turned over to where Kate sat with Lilly.

As he expected, Kate looked up, saw that it was Summer, and then glanced over at him, her brows raised.

He nodded. He was pretty sure that she was asking if he could take Lilly for a little bit so Summer could talk. He was guessing, since Summer ran a counseling equine therapy program, that Kate was probably wanting to talk to her to see if there was anything that she could do for Lilly. Kate was diligent about doing her homework and leaving no stone unturned. It didn't surprise him at all that she might be talking to Summer.

A couple of minutes later, Lilly came over to him.

He smiled at his daughter and gave her some ribbon so she could tie a few bows onto the cellophane. His daughter had a natural knack for making things look pretty, very much like Lauren did. Lilly reminded him so much of Lauren in so many ways that sometimes he wondered if she was cloned, because he had trouble seeing anything of himself in her. Except for her honey blonde hair. It was just a shade or two lighter than his own and would probably darken to match his by the time she was an adult.

Regardless, she had her mother's eyes, her nose, her flair for making things beautiful, and she seemed to have a strong interest in the candy cane shop. But sometimes he wondered if that was just because it was what he did. His brother had suggested more than once that Lilly was interested in the candy cane shop because of Jack, not because of Lauren. Since kids had a tendency to be interested in what their parents were interested in, and since Jack was the only parent Lilly had, it was natural that she would be interested in his interests.

Bryan had said that perhaps if Jack had been farming, Lilly's interest would have been there.

Jack supposed Bryan had a point, but he hadn't been able to move himself out of the candy cane shop, just because... he supposed because Lauren was dead and couldn't talk to him about it. And he didn't want Lilly not to have a part of her heritage.

Summer and Kate talked for about twenty minutes, then Kate

stood and walked Summer to the door. They chatted the entire way, with Summer calling a goodbye to Jack before she disappeared out the door.

Jack was antsy to hear what Summer had said, but he didn't want to talk about it in front of Lilly, and indeed, Kate just came over, thanked him for keeping an eye on her, and then asked Lilly if she would like to go back to the table.

This time when they sat down, Kate took the music box off the shelf and set it on the table.

Immediately, Jack could see Lilly's eyes light up as she recognized the small box.

He castigated himself for not bringing it out sooner, since it wasn't sadness that lit Lilly up, but excitement and happiness.

Kate said something, although Jack was too far away to hear what it was, but Lilly nodded eagerly as Kate opened the lid, and the music box started to play.

If Lilly was happy before, she was absolutely animated now. Her eyes bright, her cheeks flushed, her finger gently stroking the side of the music box as it played a little tune.

It slowly wound down, and then Jack's heart stopped. It looked like, as Lilly looked up at Kate, she opened her mouth, and Jack's breath hitched. Was she going to speak?

It sure looked like she was, but at the last moment, Lilly looked at the music box and then tapped it.

If Jack wasn't mistaken, a little bit of the air went out of Kate as well, and he bet she had also been thinking that Lilly was going to speak.

But Kate nodded and said, "Do you want me to play it again?"

Lilly nodded eagerly.

They listened to the music box and stayed in the corner until it was time for Lilly to go up for bedtime. As he put her to bed, he talked about the music box, and her eyes brightened again. But there were no more almost-breakthrough moments where she almost spoke.

Jack walked back down the stairs with excitement, but also disappointment. And he didn't understand the disappointment. After all, she had almost spoken. That was real progress. But what if that was the only progress she made? What if she never actually got to the point where she stepped across the line and finally spoke words?

It was hard for him to keep up the optimism that eventually she would speak.

As he walked in, Kate was where he had left her, washing dishes. It was one of his least favorite jobs, and she had volunteered to do whatever he needed her to.

"I'm sorry I left you here washing dishes," he said, knowing that while he did it, he didn't enjoy it.

"I kind of like washing dishes. It's a mindless task that allows your brain to wander, and you can figure things out while you've got the suds and the soap and the lack of anything that you actually have to think about."

"I hadn't thought about it like that, but maybe I just don't have anything to think about, and that's why it bothers me so bad."

She smiled, but then her eyes brightened. "Did you see Lilly tonight? Boy, I thought she was going to actually speak the words to ask me to play it again. That was a really brilliant idea of yours."

"You know, I don't know why I haven't done it before, other than I thought the memories would be sad. That was her mother's."

"There's definitely a key there. Obviously, she stopped speaking after her mother died, but every time we get something of hers out, or draw a picture—it's just everything revolves around her. That's the key."

"Did Summer shed any insight on that?" he asked, as he walked over and grabbed the towel to dry the dishes off before they started something new.

Kate finished washing a dish before she spoke, holding the clean bowl over the water absentmindedly as she seemed to think about the words as they came out. "I think Summer thought I was doing a pretty good job. She's never worked with someone with Lilly's specific issue, but she said that just having her use her senses, the way I was—like with the drawing, and then with music, and just making sure that Lilly was able to trust me." She lifted her shoulder. "It was really encouraging, though, because she said there'll be little gains, maybe some losses, but eventually the breakthrough would happen. She phrased it in those terms and didn't give any room for the 'what if it doesn't,' which is sometimes what goes through my head."

"Mine too. In fact, today, when she almost spoke, I was excited, but I was also discouraged as well, I guess. Because that was my exact thought. What if that's as far as she ever gets?"

"Well, Summer said something else that really got me thinking. She said, 'What if she never speaks? Is that really going to be so bad?'" She sighed and then looked up at Jack, meeting his eyes. "I know you're her parent, and maybe it would be a terrible thing for you, but I was just thinking, it's not that bad. Sure, I'd like to see her speak. I think life would be better for her if she were able to communicate that way with people, but... why do we always insist that whatever is wrong needs to be fixed? Why can't we just be happy with the other things that we have? She's healthy, she's doing well in school, she has friends, even though she doesn't talk, and she's got a really awesome dad who cares about her deeply and who is sacrificing his own dreams to make sure that she has the heritage that was given to her by a mother who obviously adored her as well. She has so many things going for her, and yet all of us are focused on the one thing that she doesn't have, which is speech."

Jack was speechless. Literally. He had never even considered that.

"What if someone just focused on my faults? I've got a bunch of them, and what if that was what everyone saw when they looked at me? What if that was what everyone was trying to make better? Not that we shouldn't try to help someone who needs it. It's just..."

"I totally get what you're saying. We have a tendency to focus on the negative."

"Exactly. And kind of parallel to that, it's a belief that I've held for a while, and that is that a person can be happy, no matter what their circumstances are. It's like the joy of the Lord—we have it with us all the time; sometimes we just choose to look at how terrible everything is, and we forget that we have a choice. The choice to be happy, the choice to be content, like Paul talked about. We just want to get things fixed first."

That hit Jack hard. She hadn't said it in so many words, but in the back of his head, he was resentful that he had to give up his farming dreams and do the candy cane shop. But could he really be happy being a candy maker for the rest of his life? Could he give up the farm completely?

The idea was novel, and he figured he would need to think about it, but in reality, Kate was right.

"The Bible says, 'Whatsoever thy hand findeth to do, do it with thy might.' And you're right, Paul says to be content in whatsoever state you are. We're also supposed to focus on the good things, the true and lovely things, and yet in my life, and with my daughter, I've been focusing on the things I don't have."

"I think that's a natural human tendency, which is probably why we needed the command in the Bible. We needed something to tell us that we're focusing on the wrong thing and to shift our eyes to where we need to focus, which is Jesus first, because when we look at Jesus, all of the other things that seem so pressing and urgent kind of fade away."

"Definitely. They definitely do."

He was quiet for a while, just thinking, thoughts turning in his head. Kate had really shifted the way he had been thinking and the way he knew he needed to see things.

What if he put his whole heart and mind and soul into loving candy making? What if he went all in on candy canes? What if he sold his half of the farm to his brother and chose to be happy right where he was?

The idea was so foreign to him that he almost recoiled from it.

But this was what God had given him to do. Couldn't he do it with all his might? Couldn't he do it with the joy of the Lord? Couldn't he do it with contentment and happiness?

The rest of the evening was fun companionship as they finished up the dishes, and then he started showing Kate simple candy-making techniques. He knew that she would be completely new to everything, so he'd chosen the simplest of the heritage candy canes to start on, and by the time midnight rolled around, they had three batches finished and wrapped and ready for display.

"That's a really nice thing about candy canes. They don't go bad, and they don't get old. So those can sit there for as long as we need them to."

Kate untied the apron that he'd given her and pushed her hair back with her other hand. "They're so pretty, I almost hate the thought of anyone eating them. I feel like we should just sit here and look at them."

There seemed to be a warm, happy atmosphere in the shop, even though they were probably the only ones still open on the street. He hadn't turned the sign or locked the door, but they hadn't had a customer since Lilly had gone to bed.

"I've had a really good time tonight." That was probably inappropriate. Not only was she helping him in the shop, but she was also working with his daughter. He probably needed to maintain a more professional distance. "And we got a lot of work done. That's such a relief. I felt like I was drowning in all the things I needed to do, and now I feel like I have breathing room."

Maybe she wanted him to say more—he wasn't sure, because she had looked a little disappointed when he shifted the tone of his conversation—but surely she would want to keep things professional as well. He didn't know if the school had any protocols about employees dating or being involved with the parents of their clients' kids, but he didn't want to get Kate in trouble. Not when she had just moved to Mistletoe Meadows.

"I better get going. I didn't realize it was almost midnight." She sounded a little breathless, and he wondered about that too.

"Thank you." He wanted to go on and on, but he didn't want to keep her, although he didn't want her to leave either.

"I appreciate being here. I've never looked at candy making from quite this perspective before, and it's new and fun, especially when you finish and you have a product that is as beautiful as those are." She nodded at the candy canes that sat on the counter.

"I suppose when you say it like that, it is a pretty awesome job."

Her eyes narrowed, as though she were trying to see what was behind his words. He wasn't even sure himself, although their conversation from earlier in the evening ran loud in his head. He wanted to be content. He wanted to do what God had given him and not insist that he needed to do what he wanted. Still, the idea of giving up farming was hard, but it was like Kate said—making candy canes was definitely rewarding. He just hadn't been focusing on the right thing.

"Do me a favor and text me when you get home. I hate the thought that you're leaving here so late, and something might happen."

"I'll text you. It only takes about ten minutes to get out there, and you should be hearing from me shortly." She smiled. "Have a good evening." With her hand on the door, she paused for a moment, before, with a jingle of the bells above it, she disappeared.

He stood in the shop—the warm atmosphere, the soft lighting, the scent of sugar and candy in the air, and the beautiful wrapped candy all around him—made him feel warm and cozy and happy. Happy in a way he hadn't for a long time. Maybe lighter too.

Lord, I think you knew just what I needed when you sent Kate into my life. I needed a perspective change; I needed to be looking at you instead of myself. I needed... I needed some fun and laughter too. Thank you.

Chapter Fourteen

"Thank you all for coming. I know we all have important things to do, so I'll try to keep this brief." Marjorie McBride stood in front of a small circle of chairs, where the members of the town Christmas festival meeting were seated.

Kate sat beside Marjorie as her helper and had her laptop open, intending to take notes.

She tried not to allow her gaze to stray toward Jack, who sat almost directly across from her. He looked especially handsome this evening with his hair combed back. Although cut short, there were a few errant ends that curled up, giving him a slightly boyish look. It softened the angles of his face and made him more endearing.

"So we have all the previous years' blueprints to go by, but of course we would like to do something a little bit new and different this year." Marjorie smiled at Kate. "Kate, I know you're new here, but I thought you had an excellent idea, and I was wondering if you'd like to stand and present it to the group?" Marjorie looked back around at the rest of the group. "We need to come up with a theme first, before we can think about what kind of decorations we want to do. We also need to pass it on to the vendors and store owners who will be involved, so they can play into the theme if they would like."

Kate stood, smiling at Marjorie and feeling slightly encouraged by her support.

Not that the townspeople had been hostile in any way to her. Quite the contrary. As she had worked with Jack for the last almost week, people had been very, very friendly. She'd had the same kind of reception at the school as well. Still, she was very conscious of her position as a newcomer. Sometimes newcomer ideas were not well tolerated.

"Thank you all for your attention. When Marjorie and I were discussing this, I suggested a Mistletoe Meadows heritage theme to showcase our local businesses and the history that our town has. Also, there's tons of history with anything Christmas, and I thought we could maybe bring that all together." It was a short description, but in her experience, the shorter these types of meetings were, the better. People were busy, and it was easier to get people to volunteer if they didn't think they were going to be spending half of their Christmas season sitting in a meeting, trying to figure things out.

"I thought that was a lovely idea," Marjorie said. Again, Kate felt encouraged by her presence, even though Marjorie seemed a little unsteady on her feet, and her shoulders drooped as though she were tired. There also seemed to be tightened lines around her face and deep shadows around her eyes.

Her daughter, Terry, was the town doctor, and Kate was sure that Terry had her finger on the pulse of whatever was ailing her.

Unless, of course, she was busy with her pregnancy, about to welcome a new baby into the world.

That had a tendency to take a person's full attention, as Kate well knew. Not that she had children of her own, but she'd seen it over and over again with kids in her care at school. When a mother was expecting, that mother seemed to think about everything in terms of babies and bottles and diapers and all the preparations that went with them, not to mention the uncomfortableness of pregnancy and the lack of sleep. She could go on and on.

So maybe she shouldn't say anything about Marjorie. But she didn't know to whom or what she should even say. Just that the woman looked tired? Everyone did around the holidays, didn't they?

As the meeting progressed, the other committee members seemed to be really enthused about her idea, and they came up with a lot of ideas, not just with decorations for the festival, but advertising as well, which was exceptionally important, and they needed to get on that immediately.

They all had some ideas for Jack too, whose shop would be the featured shop, and they wanted to make sure that there was plenty of visibility for him. The shop owners took turns being featured, and everyone knew that it was in their best interest to do their best for him, so that when it was their turn, the whole town pitched in again.

"Well, I think that about wraps it up," Marjorie said, although now she leaned on the podium rather than stood behind it.

She opened her mouth to say something else, but then, almost so quickly Kate missed it, she simply fell to the floor.

There was a collective gasp in the room before several of the men rushed forward, including her son Gilbert, and Amy and Jones, her daughter and son-in-law. All three of them were at the meeting and were at Marjorie's side in an instant.

Kate stood back, ready to do something if needed, but having absolutely no idea what to do to help Marjorie, other than pull her phone out and dial 911. She had it in her hand when Jones looked up, saw her holding her phone, and said, "Please dial 911."

Perfect timing. She did so, and seconds later, she was able to tell them that an ambulance had been dispatched and was on its way.

Not long after that, Terry burst into the room.

"Mom?" she said, as she moved forward toward the cluster of people, although probably not able to actually see her mother amid the crowd.

They parted for her to get through, and Kate stepped back as well.

"I think I'm fine," Marjorie said, although her voice sounded weak.

"Mother. Please stay right there. Is there an ambulance on the way?" Terry said, already kneeling beside her mother.

There were murmurs of assent, and Kate said, "I just spoke with the dispatcher. They said five minutes."

"All right. Thank you for loosening her clothing. Did she hit anything when she fell? Could there be a back injury?"

"Terry, I'm fine. My legs work just fine, my back doesn't hurt at all, and I need to finish this meeting!"

"Mom?" Roland and Nelly burst into the building and hurried forward toward the cluster of people.

"She collapsed just a few minutes ago, and an ambulance has already been called. But she's talking and said she could move everything just fine." Kate gave them an update, and they stopped in front of her, unable to reach their mother through the cluster of other people.

"Thank goodness. I have been concerned about her for a while. She just doesn't seem like herself," Roland said. "I've been chalking it up to her new diabetes diagnosis, but..."

"We're concerned it might be something more serious," Nelly said low, so only Kate could hear.

Kate nodded. She had a feeling it was a little bit more than diabetes too, unless Marjorie wasn't managing it very well, which, considering how dependable and responsible Marjorie was, she couldn't imagine that was the case.

"All right. Everyone, please step back," two uniformed emergency workers said as they stepped into the building, rolling a gurney between them.

The crowd parted, and Kate stepped back as well. She hated to just stand there doing nothing, but she wanted to be available in case someone needed her.

"Kate! I need to talk to Kate!" Marjorie's voice rang out over the murmur of other low voices.

"I'm right here, Miss Marjorie," Kate said, stepping forward and touching Marjorie so that her eyes were drawn to Kate.

"I need you to take over as head of the committee. I don't want the Christmas festival to suffer just because something happened to me."

"I will take over until you're able to do it again. But I'm not going to be the head of the committee if this is just a small issue."

"I think there might be something more seriously wrong with her. I know it will ease her mind if you'll just go ahead and run the committee until she's able to get back." Terry spoke low and seriously, but her affection for her mother was clear.

"I'll do whatever I need to do. But the position is always open for you to step back in, okay?" Kate said, lifting her brows at Marjorie.

Marjorie nodded, and then she looked at the medical professionals. "Now you can take me away. But be careful—I don't want to arrive at the hospital looking like I've been through a windstorm."

The crowd laughed as Marjorie patted her hair.

Kate stepped back as the EMTs wheeled Marjorie out, her children following in a large group.

Finally, the door was shut, with fewer people left than they'd begun with.

"All right, everyone, I think we were pretty much done anyway. If you have any questions or have any great ideas, please feel free to make sure you call or text me." She gave her phone number and noticed several people writing it down.

"I heard Marjorie putting you in charge. Should we check in with you until further notice?" Jack spoke from across the circle.

"Yes. Please. I think for now we shouldn't be bothering Marjorie, although once she's well enough, we definitely need to include her. Someone who's been as involved as she has will feel left out and perhaps a little lonely if she's suddenly dropped from the committee entirely." She couldn't imagine being Marjorie, who was used to immersing herself in everything, and now all of a sudden needed to take it easy. No wonder she was struggling.

"That's very considerate of you," Olivia said, and the others nodded approvingly. It was obvious that Marjorie was a well-loved member of the community.

"Before we go, I think it would be a good idea for us to pray for Marjorie," Kate said. She wasn't used to taking a stand and being a spiritual leader, but it seemed like the right thing to do. After all, everyone at the meeting attended church regularly, and it was good for Christians to pray together.

Her announcement was met with resounding approval, and she looked at Jack.

He gave a slightly perceptible nod, and she said, "If Jack would stand and pray for us and also dismiss the meeting, please?"

He nodded again and stood.

His prayer was short but heartfelt, and soon the meeting had adjourned.

Kate felt like it had been a whirlwind. She'd started the meeting thinking she was just going to give Marjorie a hand, and now she ended it with the weight of the town Christmas festival on her shoulders, which did not feel strong enough to handle it all. But she would have to, because there was no one else. She could step up and do it, and once more, despite her difficult financial situation, she was grateful that her job didn't start officially until after the holidays. It was perfect timing, because it gave her plenty of time to work on whatever she needed to work on.

God had known all along that she was going to need that time, and she loved the way He had worked things out.

She spoke with all the committee members and felt like everyone had a handle on what they needed to do. It had been a productive meeting, even if it had not gone quite the way she had anticipated.

"You did a wonderful job. And I know you're going to be fine as the head of the committee." She turned to see Jack standing behind her, as the last of the other committee members walked out the door.

"I don't know if I feel up to the task. In fact, I feel rather intimidated."

"If you felt confident, I might be a little concerned. It's always good to have a little bit of insecurity. That drives us to be better and keeps us from being overconfident and arrogant."

"I suppose you're right. But I would feel a little better if I had someone like Marjorie to learn under before I had to take it over myself."

"I'm sure you're going to be fine. It's probably better this way. This way you don't have preconceived notions about how you have to do it, but you can feel free to let your creativity loose, without unconsciously trying to stick to the way we've always done it." He paused for a minute and then gave her a little smile. "Weren't we just talking about how it doesn't matter how things actually go—we can be happy and joyful no matter what?"

"You're right. This is not really what I was thinking when I was talking to you about that, but I guess God's timing is perfect. And you're looking on the bright side, seeing the most positive spin, and I appreciate that."

She appreciated the fact that he challenged her to live the way she said she believed, and not just allow her to talk the talk, but pushed her to walk the walk as well.

"You know, I had really been thinking about that since you and I talked a few days ago in the shop that night."

"Yeah?" she said, as Jack shifted on his feet.

"I had been allowing my thoughts to go in a negative direction, and it kept me from being content where I was. It's true that I'll always love farming, but it's also true that I really do enjoy making candy. I just... resented the fact that I didn't have a choice about it, instead of looking at all the positive benefits and keeping my mind focused on those."

"There's so much that we can do right around us. It's silly for any of us to be so down about our own circumstances when we could be looking around at people we could help."

They stood there for a moment, and then they both seemed to realize it was getting late.

"I better go. Do you want me to walk you to your car?"

Kate's eyes widened. She wasn't expecting that.

Jack almost looked like he wanted to take it back. Or maybe it was her imagination. He put a hand up.

"Never mind. I guess it's just gentlemanly chivalry that comes out every once in a while. I know you're perfectly capable of walking to your own car. And it's not that late."

"Mistletoe Meadows is perfectly safe."

"It sure is. You did a great job tonight. I'm glad you're in charge. Thank you."

"Good night, Jack," she said, wondering what made him change his mind. Was it her? Did he want to be nice, and so therefore forced himself to do a little bit more than what he normally would? Or was he just not interested in her the way she seemed to be interested in him, since her eyes couldn't help but go to him anytime they were in the same room together?

Whatever it was, she ended up watching him walk out, turning just before he closed the door, in case he looked back. But as far as she knew, he didn't.

Chapter Fifteen

"I hope we're not interrupting anything," Jack said cautiously as he stepped outside Marjorie's hospital room, where Roland and Nelly stood, talking softly together.

Roland's head came up, and his eyes widened, and then his face broke out into a grin when he recognized Jack.

"Of course not. You're always welcome."

"Lilly was concerned about our Sunday school teacher, so she drew her a picture, and I figured that we'd just swing by on the way home from school."

There were very few beds in the new Medical Center, and they couldn't take acute patients, but Marjorie's condition had been deemed low enough risk that they kept her overnight instead of sending her to the bigger hospital in Harrisonburg.

"I'm sure that will cheer her up immensely. She hates being cut off from all of the things that she feels like she should be doing this time of year," Nelly said, smiling gently at Lilly, who clutched the paper she'd drawn that morning before school to her chest.

"Is she awake?" Jack asked.

"Yes, awake and begging the doctors to allow her to go home.

They hadn't made a decision about that when Nelly and I needed to step out for business not related to my mother," Roland said with a smile.

"Good to know," Jack said, as Roland opened the door. He took Lilly's hand, and they stepped in slowly.

Marjorie's eyes came up, and she smiled, looking truly pleased to see them.

"My goodness, look who's come to see me!" she said, a hand to her chest, her eyes on Lilly.

Lilly held up the picture that she had drawn. Jack figured it was too much to hope that Lilly would speak, even though she loved Marjorie with all of her little heart. Marjorie made Sunday school fun, and Lilly couldn't wait to go on Sunday mornings.

"Oh my goodness, look at this. Is this for me?" Marjorie asked, reaching out a hand that was still connected to an IV, the tubes following her, and Lilly's eyes got hooked on them.

"Those are just to make sure that Miss Marjorie is getting all the nutrients she needs. Sometimes when you're sick, you don't feel like eating."

Jack turned to see Kate walking, taking the final step toward Lilly and kneeling down beside her, putting her arm around the little girl.

Jack didn't need a magnifying glass to see Lilly relax and even give a tremulous smile at Kate's presence and words.

"These things? Were they scaring you?" Marjorie said. "I'm sorry. I never even thought about that."

"She just looks a little different in the hospital than she does at Sunday school, doesn't she?"

Lilly nodded, her little head going up and down like that was exactly what she had been thinking. How did Kate do that? Just get inside his daughter's head, figure out what was bothering her, and think of something to say to ease her fears?

Kate was obviously very good at her job. And the fact that she was taking a special interest in Lilly warmed his heart. If anyone could get Lilly to talk again, it would be Kate.

But then he reminded himself of what he had already figured out —it didn't matter if Lilly ever spoke again. He would love her, no matter what. Yes, he thought it would be better for her to speak, but there were so many things about his daughter that were amazing, and maybe the fact that she wasn't speaking would help her develop some of the things that God needed for her to be able to use at some point in her life. After all, everything happened for a reason, and there definitely was a reason for his daughter not speaking.

Maybe... maybe it was to bring Kate into his life.

He almost scoffed aloud at that thought, as Kate and Marjorie and Lilly continued to have a bit of a lopsided conversation, since Lilly added nothing to it.

There was nothing between Kate and him, and there wouldn't be. Kate would make sure of it. She would not risk her job at the school, and she really wouldn't be interested in a candy maker anyway. Especially a candy maker who wasn't even sure his candy-making operation was going to be in business next year this time. He had nothing to offer her. Well, he supposed he did offer her the farmhouse, but that wasn't all his. It was his brother's, and he was seriously thinking about selling out. If he sold his half of the farm, he would have more money to invest in the candy-making business and could do the improvements that he had been thinking about for a while. He'd be able to buy the storage building behind his shop and perhaps hire some workers, or even put a kitchen in that building and ship all across the United States next year.

He could really expand his candy-making business, but that would mean letting go of his farm dream.

Was that really a dream? Or was it just an image he liked to think of himself having?

"And I'm hoping to get out of here so that I can be at Sunday school with you on Sunday," Marjorie said, as Jack shook his head and tried to focus on the conversation in front of him. These two ladies were doing everything in their power to include his daughter and make her feel good. He appreciated them more than he could say.

"I'm sure she will be. You're looking very good," Kate said.

Just then the doctor walked in, and Jack took Lilly's hand.

"We better go, so that Miss Marjorie can talk to her doctor and maybe talk the doc into letting her out of here."

"We're going to look at your numbers and make sure that you're better before we let you go. We don't want anything to happen to Miss Marjorie. Mistletoe Meadows would never be the same, and I wouldn't forgive myself," the doctor smiled, and Kate stood as well.

"Take care of yourself, Miss Marjorie," Kate said.

"I will. When I get out of here, I would like for you to stop by my house, and we can talk about what's been going on with the festival."

"Absolutely. You just let me know when."

Kate smiled, and they all waved at Miss Marjorie as they filed out of the door.

"She does look a lot better," Jack said as he closed the door softly behind them.

Roland and Nelly had disappeared, and it was just Kate and Lilly and him in the hall.

"I thought so. Although it does bother me that they don't seem to be able to figure out what the problem was, and they need to run more tests. At least that's what Roland and Nelly told me when I walked in. Did you hear anything different?" Kate said, her voice low and concerned.

"No, I hadn't," he said, pressing his lips together. "I do hope that they find it, though. There's nothing more frustrating than knowing that there's something wrong with you but being unable to figure out what."

"It's like a mystery. And sometimes it's like a mystery where you don't have all the clues. Very frustrating."

They started walking down the short hall. The hospital wasn't very big. It was more like a Medical Center with a few rooms where patients could be kept overnight. Mistletoe Meadows would like to expand it, but they were happy that they had been able to get this much done. As small a town as they were, it was good to have a place where people could go without having to travel over the mountains.

"I see we both had the same idea."

"Stop in and see Miss Marjorie after school?" Kate asked with a twinkle in her eye.

"Exactly."

"Great minds think alike," she said, quoting the old saying.

"I guess they do."

Jack looked down, and it was then that he realized that Lilly held both of their hands, the way a child might hold the hand of her mother and the hand of her father as she walked between them.

Kate must have realized that at the same time, because she gently disengaged her hand from Lilly's as she opened the door to the outside, using that as an excuse.

"I was on my way to your shop, so I guess this is perfect timing, meeting you here. I was going to text you and let you know that I would be late, but I ended up on a call with one of the teachers at the school and didn't have time."

"Obviously it doesn't matter, since I was here. And same—I was going to text you, then I picked up Lilly, and we were making sure that we had the picture that she wanted to give Marjorie completely finished, and I forgot."

"Well, it turns out that was okay, since we both met here and we didn't need to let each other know."

"Funny how that worked out," he said, thinking again about what they had been saying—that everything happened for a reason.

Sometimes, it was just hard to figure out why.

Chapter Sixteen

On Monday, Kate told Jack she would be late to the candy shop since she needed to stop by Marjorie's house first. Marjorie had come home on Friday and made it to church on Sunday, even teaching her Sunday school class, although her daughter, Amy, had helped her a good bit.

Regardless, Kate admired the woman for her grit and determination, but also her cheerful attitude.

She wondered if she would be able to respond in such a positive way if her health was not what she wanted it to be. She had a feeling that that was something that she would have to work on.

Maybe Marjorie could give her some pointers—not that she had any intention of getting sick, but she suspected that it wasn't something that happened at the moment of sickness, but was something that had been cultivated years before.

Determining that she would ask Marjorie about it if they had time after discussing the town Christmas festival, she stepped up to the door and knocked.

"Come on in," a voice called from the other side of the door.

It sounded like Marjorie, upbeat and cheerful as always, even through the door.

Kate turned the knob, and indeed, it was unlocked.

She stepped in, looking around at the slightly messy but warm and cozy kitchen.

Somehow, even though there was nothing expensive or fancy about it, the kitchen looked like home, with several pictures obviously drawn by children tacked to the door of the refrigerator. Kate was able to pick out the picture Lilly had drawn. There were dried flowers in a vase above one cupboard, and there was flour on the counter and a bowl with a towel over top of it, as though bread were rising. The kitchen still sparkled and smelled like cinnamon and sugar, and gave a person a warm, homey feeling that only happened in the most real of homes.

"Walking in here just feels like coming home," Kate said, before she could stop herself. She had never really walked into a house that smelled like this, and she didn't know why this one felt like home to her. It shouldn't. TV dinners and silence usually greeted her when she walked in when she lived with her parents. Even now, it was quiet and still when she walked into the farmhouse, as it had been when she walked into her apartment in Baltimore.

She noted two casserole dishes sitting on the counter and a vase of fresh flowers sitting on the table. A sack of potatoes sat on one chair, and what looked like sweet potatoes sat in a box beside them.

"You must have just gone grocery shopping," Kate said, without thinking.

"Oh goodness no, I don't think I'm up to that," Marjorie said, in the first comment that Kate had heard that she wasn't feeling quite herself. "It's just the town showering me with love. In small towns, casseroles and/or food usually mean love."

"I'll keep that in mind," Kate said.

"Also, I've gotten several vases of flowers, and Ben gave me potatoes from his garden. Olivia grows the best sweet potatoes in Virginia, and that's what's in the box there."

"And Bryan sends his love, because the way a farmer shows love is by giving a person a big piece of bloody meat. It's in the fridge."

Kate laughed. "I'm not sure that would make me feel loved," she said, unable to suppress a shudder.

"That's a farmer for you," Marjorie said with a wave of her hand. "They're a little different than the rest of us," she winked.

"Well, it's good to know, in case that ever happens to me. If someone had given me a piece of big bloody meat, I might question whether or not they even liked me."

"No. That's true love," Marjorie waved her hand around. "Do you want to sit at the bar, or would you like to sit at the table?"

"Wherever it's most comfortable for you."

"Well, I have bread rising—I'm going to need to work it—so if you don't mind, we can sit here at the bar, and I can jump up and punch that thing down whenever it's ready."

"That sounds kind of energetic for a person who had just been in the hospital a few days ago."

"There's something about doing bread that's therapeutic for the soul. It doesn't really matter how sick you are; it still makes you feel better."

"I don't know if I've ever made homemade bread before."

"I personally love sourdough, but I gave all my starter away, and I need to make some more. This is just regular yeast bread."

"Sourdough bread sounds good too." She wanted to do all of those things, but it was an awful lot for a person to do and still work a full-time job. Plus, she was working a little extra to pay for her living place; she really didn't have time to bake bread, although that seemed like such a soul-soothing job.

"I really appreciate you coming out. I know this is a little out of your way."

"It was worth it to step through the door and smell all those delicious smells and just feel the atmosphere here. You make it feel like a home."

"I think it's God that makes a home, although I suppose I know a lot of people who claim to be Christians, and you don't feel that peace and comfort when you walk into their house."

"No," Kate agreed, wondering how people felt when they walked into her home.

They chatted for a bit more before Marjorie settled herself on a stool beside Kate.

They talked about the festival, and Kate laid out all the things that had been happening. She had specifically called everyone who was involved to get the latest updates, so that Marjorie didn't miss a thing.

She was pretty sure that Marjorie appreciated it, because the lady loved to be involved in things.

"You know, I expected you to be a little bit more down. But you're not bitter; you're not angry; you don't seem frustrated... you just seem happy." Kate pushed the papers aside, and Marjorie, with her hands in the bread dough, looked up in surprise.

"Because I am having some physical difficulties?"

"Yeah. Someone like you, who's used to running around everywhere and doing whatever you want, to be laid up, to be held back, especially this time of year. I thought I would see you more flustered or upset or something. I don't know."

Marjorie stopped for a moment, looking off into the distance, as though gathering her thoughts.

"Well, sometimes God has a tendency to test you on things that you think you have a handle on, so I don't want you to think that I know everything. But I think the more you get to know God, the closer you are to Him, the more you're willing to let yourself and your own agenda go. And the more content you are with what you have and what you've been given, whether that's material possessions or your lot in life, so to speak. The things that you can't do anything about, even if you wanted to, like your health, and even, to a certain extent, your family."

Kate nodded. That made sense. She couldn't change her parents;

she just had to be happy with the parents that God gave her and accept them for what they were and try to love them no matter what. That made sense.

"But how do you know God? How do you get closer to Him?" She paused for a moment. "I want to be like that. I want to be the kind of person who lives my Christian talk, but I don't know how."

Marjorie's brows lifted, and then her eyes narrowed. Kate liked the fact that she wasn't just zipping off a quick, random answer, but she seemed to really be thinking about Kate's question.

"You have to read your Bible. You have to do it on a daily basis. And not just a verse, not just a quick 'I did my reading for the day,' but immerse yourself in it. When you wash your hands, you don't just take two drops of water and say that's enough. No, you run the water over in large quantities, so that you're sure you get them clean. That's what you do with the Bible—you dig into it in large quantities, so that you're sure to get enough, because it washes your soul clean. It washes your insides, cleans the bad stuff out, kind of acts like a filter."

"A lot? What do you mean by a lot?"

"Well, in my opinion, a Christian should definitely be reading their Bible through. Whether it's in a year or in two years or in three years, I don't know, but you should be reading the entire thing. God gave it all to us for a reason."

"But there are whole chapters that I don't even begin to understand. Like Isaiah. It goes on and on forever, and I have no clue what he's even talking about." Kate lifted her hands and then allowed them to drop back down on the counter.

But Marjorie just laughed. "That's me when I first started reading. I didn't understand half of what I was reading. But the fact of the matter is, you're in the Bible, you're reading it. Eventually it will make sense to you. You pray, and you ask God for wisdom, and sometimes you can go to commentaries or online and look up YouTube channels, but that's the other thing you need to do—talk to

God about it. Ask the Holy Spirit to show you. If you're a Christian, the Holy Spirit is inside of you. But the Holy Spirit can't show you without you at least reading for yourself. It's not like He's going to drop the knowledge into your head. You have to go after it. And so much of the Bible instructs on the Bible. So if you're only reading, say, Matthew, Mark, Luke, and John, which are easier, and the rest of the New Testament, which is definitely easier than the Old Testament, you're missing things that you need in order to put the pieces together. You need to read the whole thing; you need to read a lot of it; you need to read it often. You need to have a daily time where you're talking to God, reading the Bible, and absorbing it." Marjorie paused. "That's not to say that you shouldn't meditate on one or two verses."

"Is that what you do?"

"Well, I've been doing this for a while, so don't think that you're going to just start being perfect overnight. Not that I'm perfect by any stretch," she said, slapping the bread around and then forming it into a ball. "But what I do is, I'm on a schedule to read my Bible through in a year. So I read that first. And then I pray, and sometimes I pray before I read, just to ask God to show me what He wants me to learn. I'll take notes, copy out verses—it's not a quick process. I take at least a half an hour, and sometimes even double that. And then I have verses that I'm memorizing. Those are the verses that I think about, kind of chew on, work on throughout the day. Those are the verses that I'm putting into my memory. Because the Bible says I need to hide His word in my heart so that I won't sin against Him. God obviously wants us to memorize the Bible. So I work a little day after day. As I get older, it's gotten a little bit harder, but it's also true that the more you do it, the better you get at it. Like anything else."

Marjorie gave her a small smile. "Does that answer your question?"

"Yeah, it really does. But I don't know where to start."

"I do think there's a place for Christian books and Christian teachings and all of that. And you definitely want to be in church.

You learn a lot from church, but you need to make sure that the pastor is opening up the Bible and teaching directly from it. Expository teaching is best, but if he gives a sermon on Sunday morning and does expository teaching on Sunday night, you're getting both. And that's good too."

"So you do think that reading good books on the Bible is okay?"

"Absolutely. But the more that you're in the Bible, the more you can look at those books and go, 'Oh, I don't agree with that,' or 'I think they've got it wrong here,' or 'They said this, but they didn't back that up with the Bible, and I don't think that's right.'"

"I see. So you read those books to be encouraged and challenged, but you also read them using the Bible as your yardstick, making sure they line up with it?"

"That's exactly right. That's what you need to do." Marjorie smiled. "Now, it's my turn to ask you a couple of questions."

"All right," Kate said, putting her hands up as though she were willing to answer whatever Marjorie asked her.

"Are you settling into town okay? Are you happy at the farmhouse? And how are things going with Jack and Lilly? I've heard that you've been working with them. There, how's that for firing a bunch of questions off at you?"

Kate laughed. "I don't know if I can remember them all. But I can answer the easiest ones first. I love the farmhouse. Love it. I wish it were mine. Except... that would be coveting, wouldn't it?"

"I think coveting is when you want something for your own, but wishing is a little bit different." Marjorie sat down in her chair with a small sigh. "But I also think it's best to be content where you are, with what you have. Sometimes that's the best way for God to see that you're ready for more."

"I'm definitely content with what I have. And if I never own a place as nice as the farmhouse, I can just assume that that's not what God has for me."

"That's the spirit. I love that, too, because the farmhouse isn't that big. You're actually content with very little."

Kate supposed she was right. It just seemed so expansive when she was outside looking at the view. It was inspiring, and it really was hard not to wish that it was hers.

"Now, about settling into the community. You've really helped with that by suggesting that I'd be your helper on this Christmas festival. I've definitely gotten to know a lot of people, and I've been enjoying my work. As for Jack... I suppose I'm a little more drawn to him than I should be."

"What do you mean by that?" Marjorie asked, sounding truly confused.

"Well, he's got a lot of memories tied up in his wife, whom he obviously loved very much."

"He did love her, I am sure of it. But Lauren was... she was a good woman, but I always felt that she had a hard time focusing on anything but the candy shop. Jack and Lilly kind of got left behind sometimes."

"Really? I would have thought from the way Lilly was acting that her mother doted on her."

"Don't get me wrong. It wasn't like she was neglected, but I think maybe Lilly is pining for what she wished she had, or maybe she hoped that she would eventually have it. I don't really know much about it, but... you can't rule that out."

"I'll keep that in mind."

"What about Jack?"

"What about him? He's... offered me a place to stay in return for me helping his daughter and working in the candy shop."

"You two seemed pretty in tune with each other. I think that's the right way I want to say it. It wasn't like every time you looked at each other, there were sparks flying the way you could see with some couples, particularly younger ones. But it was more of a mature attraction. Was I wrong about that?"

Kate stood speechless. Flabbergasted. Marjorie had said exactly what she felt, but she didn't really want to admit it.

"If you don't want to talk about it, you don't have to. I was just telling you what I thought I saw."

"Yeah. I think you saw correctly. But he doesn't seem the slightest bit interested in me. So there's that."

"That's not what I thought I saw," Marjorie said, her brows furrowing. "Is there something that he feels is coming between the two of you? That could be keeping you apart?"

"Not that I know of, except I'm not sure I'm interested in getting involved with someone who has so much baggage—his late wife, struggling with the candy shop, and also with Lilly. Although he and I have been talking about just accepting Lilly the way she is and not worrying about whether or not she ever talks."

"But it would be best for her to talk, wouldn't it?" Marjorie asked gently.

"I think it would be, but maybe God has something he needs her to go through, to learn from this, and to use eventually. I don't know. It's not that we've given up on her ever speaking; it's that we decided that we weren't just going to focus on what she didn't have."

"I think that's very wise. Very wise indeed," Marjorie said thoughtfully.

She seemed to be letting the idea of Jack go, which Kate appreciated. She didn't know what to say about Jack anyway. She couldn't deny that she was attracted to him; it did feel like a mature attraction, not the hormone-driven, "I can't keep my hands off of you" teenage or young adult type attraction.

"He's a good man, and I would love to see him settle down with someone who appreciates him."

"I'd like to think I would appreciate him, but... I think we're getting way, way, way ahead of the horse, since we're just friends, and I don't know that we'll be anything more."

"If you say so," Marjorie said. "Maybe you could ask him. Or maybe you could ask him if there's a reason why you couldn't be more?"

Kate wouldn't have even thought about doing that on her own, but when Marjorie suggested it, it sounded totally reasonable. Why wouldn't she ask him and see what he said? After all, she had wondered.

But she wouldn't want to ruin whatever kind of friendship they had. They did have a nice friendship going, and rocking the boat could ruin that. Although something told her that rocking the boat could make it even better.

Chapter Seventeen

"Merry Christmas, guys," Jack said, smiling as the children at the Children's Hospital held their candy canes, the wrapping ripped open and most of them already sucking on the sweet confections. The nurses smiled, and parents beamed at children who lifted sticky, smiling faces.

His eyes landed on Kate, who seemed to be deep in conversation with a little girl who had no hair. Lilly stuck close to her side, her eyes wide, obviously hanging on every word Kate said.

Lilly loved Kate so much. And Kate had been working diligently with her for more than two weeks, and Jack could be wrong, but he was pretty sure that Lilly had been making progress, albeit slow.

"Thank you so much for coming, Mr. Henderson. The kids always enjoy it." The director of activities at the hospital, Dr. James Martin, shook Jack's hand.

"I wouldn't miss it. I think it does more good to my heart than it does to anyone else. It definitely reminds me of the reason for the season and why I do what I do."

"These children could teach a lot of people lessons, if we just took the time to learn them."

Jack nodded, and Dr. Martin moved on.

"I'm so glad you asked me to come. This was an inspiring experience," Kate said, at his elbow, and he turned to face her. She glowed—there was no other way to say it—and he felt his heart turn over. He wanted to reach out, to touch her cheek, to share the connection with a physical gesture, but he fisted his hand close to his side and nodded.

Then his eyes dropped to Lilly, who was glowing almost as much as Kate.

With their light eyes and delicate bone structure, Kate and Lilly could be mother and daughter. He had never thought that Kate looked very much like his late wife at all, with her dark hair and more slender build, but Lilly definitely had similarities that could make them pass for relatives.

"I think you had a good time too, didn't you, kiddo?" he asked, playfully ruffling her hair as she nodded.

"Let's get home. It's going to be almost bedtime by the time we get there," he paused as he saw Lilly's downturned mouth. "But you can spend a little bit of time with Miss Kate if you want to before bed."

That immediately made Lilly smile, and he was glad he had guessed correctly.

Sometimes having a daughter that didn't speak at all was very frustrating, because he couldn't figure out what she wanted.

He supposed he could just ignore her until she decided to tell him. That might be what people did a few generations ago, but... he just couldn't bring himself to do that. Maybe if he had no other choice, but as long as he was able, he would allow her time to heal.

The ride home was fun, as they talked about the kids and their smiling faces and the reactions as they opened the candy canes. Jack really couldn't afford to give anything away, but at the same time, he believed he couldn't afford not to. After all, a person reaped what they sowed, and he couldn't expect God to give to him if he didn't give to others first. It was a test of faith, since that was the one thing that God specifically commanded his people to prove Him by.

Not to mention, it truly was more blessed to give than to receive. He didn't want to be irresponsible, giving when he owed money or anything like that, but he didn't want to be so selfish that he kept more for himself than what he truly needed.

By the time they pulled into the shop, it was only a half an hour until bedtime.

"Do you mind if we spend a little bit of time together?" Kate asked, pulling her bottom lip in and worrying it with her teeth.

"Thirty minutes is fine. I do have a big order I need to get filled, but... Lilly so looks forward to this time with you, and I do believe it's been very beneficial to her."

"I was afraid you would tell me that I needed to stop when there was no discernible progress."

"I think there is progress."

"I mean, with her not talking," Kate said, watching Lilly disappear into the front of the store, hurrying inside to get her crayons and paper out before Kate came in, so that they would have as much time to draw as possible.

"She's definitely got her mother's artistic flair."

"I'd like to hear more about her mother at some point," Kate said, and then she shook her head. "But I don't want to pry or anything."

He didn't say anything. He'd like to tell her more about Lauren, about the fact that he was not pining away for his late wife, but in fact felt like he might be falling in love with his daughter's therapist.

But he couldn't say those things. He didn't want to blur the line between employer and employee, renter and rent-ee, therapist and parent. He didn't want Kate to get in trouble either—not with the school—and he didn't want to throw any wrenches in her newfound relationship with the town.

"I thought the meeting last night went really well," he said as he opened the door for her to step in.

"I'm so glad Marjorie was able to be there. I still took copious notes, because I didn't want her to miss anything, but having her at the front was a really good idea. Gilbert made sure her water glass was filled up, and I noticed her kids pampering her every chance they got."

Kate sounded almost wistful, and it made him take a double take at her as he moved to go toward his candy counter.

"I can't figure out if you want children, or if you want to pamper your parents. But there was a longing in there somewhere."

Kate laughed but didn't answer him. She just lifted her shoulder and then turned to Lilly and sat down at the desk.

Interesting. He didn't just want to share about his life; he wanted Kate to tell him about hers.

He had a longing to know everything he could about her.

He didn't think too much more about it, though, as he tried to lose himself in the order that needed to be filled. He thought about bills and about whether or not he was even going to be able to keep the shop open, and about the conversation that he had with his brother over the weekend.

His brother had definitely been interested in purchasing his half of the farm, but he needed to get with his bankers and see if he was going to be able to swing that large of a purchase, and Jack couldn't do anything but tell him to take his time and get all of his ducks in a row. He didn't want Bryan to lose the farm because he was trying to bite off more than he could chew. But having Bryan purchase his share of the farm would give him the capital he needed in order to expand the candy shop and make it profitable for him, and something that he could pass on to Lilly if she was interested in it.

When that time came.

"Jack! Jack!" Kate's voice interrupted his thoughts, and it took him about a half a second to realize that something major had happened.

"Jack, oh my goodness, Jack, you've got to see this!"

Kate nodded at Lilly, and Lilly went running over to him, waving the paper beside her.

"What's this?" he asked, and then he saw it. Lilly had written a sentence at the bottom of the picture. That was new and exciting. The breakthrough they'd been waiting for.

As she held the paper out to him, he almost fell over when she said, "Look, Daddy."

He blinked, blinked again, and his mouth fell open.

"What is it, baby?" he asked, his words coming out through his constricted throat. His daughter had spoken the first words since her mother's funeral. He wanted to grab her, hug her, tell her how happy and proud he was, but instead, he looked where she pointed and saw what she had written.

Mommy is happy in heaven.

Reading the words hit him again, and he struggled to breathe.

"Oh my goodness, Jack," Kate said, from beside him, her hand at her throat, looking like she was about to faint.

He met her eyes, his own sharing his excitement, before he bent down and put his arm around Lilly, lifting her up, and in his excitement, he put his other arm around Kate and drew them together in a hug.

"I can't believe it. You spoke!" He pulled back, looking into Lilly's eyes, which shone with happiness.

She nodded, smiling.

"Mommy is happy in heaven," he repeated.

She nodded again, and then he pulled her and Kate even tighter against him. "You did it. She spoke." He looked down into Kate's eyes, his own he knew were glistening with tears. "You're amazing." Then he looked back at his daughter. "I love you. I'm so, so happy you spoke to me."

"I'm not sad anymore," Lilly said, smiling. And then she looked at Kate. "I love Miss Kate."

It was on the tip of his tongue to say "me too," but he stopped himself in time. Did he love her? It wasn't a question he was going to consider right now. Right now, his daughter had spoken for the first time in years, and he wanted to savor this moment.

"She's been so good to us and has spent so much time with you." He wanted to go on, but he knew he was babbling.

Lilly smiled. "God brought Miss Kate to me. I asked Him."

"You did?"

"I told him if I couldn't have my mommy back, I wanted a new mommy."

Jack's mouth dropped. It could have been uncomfortable, but Kate stepped in at that moment.

"Of course He's going to bring you a new mommy. God gives us every good gift. I'm so happy you're not sad anymore. We need to celebrate!" Kate said, her eyes sparkling.

"Yes, we need to celebrate." It was way past her bedtime, so he said, "You can stay up a little later tonight after your bath and we can talk about what fun things we want to do to celebrate."

Jack paused, and then he said, "I should take Miss Kate out for dinner to celebrate, if she'll let me." He turned questioning eyes to her.

She nodded immediately; maybe it was only because she was overcome with what had happened with Lilly. But she didn't seem to think twice.

Between them, Lilly smiled, as though that was what she wanted all along, and maybe it was. Maybe that was celebrating to her too.

They stood there for a while, Jack overcome with happiness, but it was getting late, and Lilly needed to go to school in the morning, no matter how exciting that evening had been. He had a few things he needed to say to Kate, so he said to Lilly, "I think it's time for you to go upstairs and get ready for bed. I will be up in a few minutes. We definitely have some celebrating to do, don't we?"

Lilly nodded and smiled, and then she leaned in, one arm around Kate, the other arm around Jack, and hugged them both tight, drawing them together. Jack suddenly was aware of exactly how close he was to Kate, and that his arm had been around her shoulders for a while. They were small and delicate, but felt warm under his arm. Her strawberry candy scent drifted up to his nose, and the soft brush of her hair sent tingles on his arm.

Lilly pulled away and went running for the stairs, leaving him feeling a little awkward. How did he drop his arm from her shoulder without being weird about it? Especially when he wanted to leave it there, to draw her tighter, to kiss her.

Really? Was that what he wanted?

Definitely. It was definitely what he wanted, but was it wise?

"Thank you. You've done so much for her, and for us. Your presence here has just been a real blessing this holiday season. Let me take you out to dinner to celebrate?"

He hadn't been planning on asking her out, although if he were being honest, he'd thought about it over and over and over again while he worked in the shop during the day without her, longing for the time when she would walk through the door with Lilly. She had taken to bringing Lilly home and saving him the trip. And he looked forward to both of them, equally.

"I'd love to," she said easily.

She didn't seem to hesitate or anything, and he figured he'd better ask the question that had been plaguing him.

"Is this something that's going to get you in trouble with your job?"

"Going out to eat with you to celebrate Lilly's progress?" she asked, sounding truly puzzled.

"Yeah. Are there some kind of rules about dating clients or anything?"

"Well, if I were dating Lilly, it might be an issue, but Lilly's dad... I don't think so. I don't think the school will have any problem with that at all. In fact, I kind of feel like the community might be happy that you found someone—that you're getting out again, anyway," she added quickly, as though she didn't want to presume that she was the one for him.

He wanted to tell her that she was more "the one" than Lauren had been, but he didn't. Maybe she was just saying yes because she didn't want to ruin the evening by saying no.

Regardless, she started to move away, and he imitated her movement, allowing his hand to slide down, feeling warm skin and a brush of her fingers as he did so, her scent coming with him, and he wished he could bottle it up, hold it with him, use it to remember this moment, and this woman, and the celebration of his daughter finally speaking.

And what words. She had accepted the fact that her mother had died, was happy that she was in heaven, and was ready for a new mom—in fact, believed that God had sent Kate.

What if Kate wasn't the one? What if Kate didn't agree to be her new mom?

Was that something they needed to talk about?

Probably, but maybe not tonight.

"I need to be getting home. I have some paperwork I need to fill out for my job, and some work I need to do on the festival. Are you still okay with me cutting out now?" she asked, and he remembered belatedly that she had said that she needed to leave early tonight.

Disappointment cut through him, but then he remembered that they were going out.

"Is tomorrow okay to go out to eat?"

"I don't want to take you away from your work."

"I think we both could use a break."

"You definitely need a break. Tomorrow is fine."

"Then if it's okay with you, I'll get Mrs. Abernathy to come watch Lilly at seven, and you and I will plan on going out for a nice treat, celebration, and... I guess I have a few things I'd like to talk to you about."

"Really?" She tilted her head, as though she had no idea what he might want to say to her.

He nodded. "Yeah. I do." Maybe she'd forgotten that Lilly had said that she wanted Kate to be her new mom and thought God had done it, or maybe she was just brushing that aside. Or maybe that's what she wanted to do.

Hopefully, he would find out tomorrow.

Chapter Eighteen

So, was it a date? Or was it just that he wanted to talk to her, so he was taking her out?

Kate wasn't sure as she looked in the mirror and made sure her hair wasn't sticking out in weird directions. She was running a little late because she had gone to Marjorie McBride's house to help with the Christmas baking and to chat about the Christmas festival. Marjorie seemed to be doing well, although she also seemed tired and admitted as much.

Kate had stayed longer than she should have and had swung by the farmhouse to quickly change her clothes and check her hair before Jack arrived to pick her up.

Jack said that he was getting Mrs. Abernathy to watch Lilly and had asked her if there was anywhere in particular she would like to go.

There was a new restaurant opening in Mistletoe Meadows, but it hadn't opened yet, so they were going to the next town over.

That seemed like a date, right?

She didn't have time to think about that anymore, because the sound of gravel crunching reached her, and she gave her hair one last pat before she flipped the light switch off and hurried out of the bathroom.

Sticking her shoes on, she was able to grab the door before Jack knocked.

The bouquet of flowers he held shocked her.

"My goodness, they're beautiful." She put a hand to her throat. Maybe this really was a date.

"Almost as beautiful as you are," he said, and she couldn't help it —she laughed.

"That's a line."

He grinned. "Actually, I'd pick you over the flowers, but that's probably a line too."

She lifted a shoulder. She really didn't know and didn't care. It was sweet for him to say, although she hardly thought it was true, because the flowers were gorgeous.

"Let me get those in some water," she said, opening the door a little further so he could step in. It felt odd inviting him into his own house.

He looked around. "It looks a little different from the last time I was in here."

"I've been adding a few little touches, but I haven't wanted to spend too much money on decorations or that type of thing. I really am saving so I can get a place of my own, whether I'm renting or buying."

"There's no rush. I'm going to talk to my brother early tomorrow morning, and I'll see if he has any issues. I don't think he does, and if not, you can stay here indefinitely."

"But you said you wouldn't have work for me since your shop wouldn't be busy after the holidays."

She led him to the kitchen, where she didn't have a vase, but she pulled a mason jar out of the cupboard.

"That's true, but if things go through with my brother, I'm hoping to ramp up production, and I will definitely need some help."

"You might need full-time help," she said, casually, as she put the jar under the water spigot and filled it half full.

"True. I don't know how things are going to look. I'm a little out of my depth, but I figured that if I'm going to work on saving the candy shop, I'd better go all in on it. What's the worst that could happen?"

"You could lose it," she said, reasonably.

"Yeah. But I could lose it if I don't try. So I might as well give it my best shot, right?"

"I agree. I admire your courage and your dedication to trying to keep it in the family for Lilly."

"I realized it was for myself too."

"I thought you always wanted to be a farmer?" she asked, setting the jar of flowers down on the counter and admiring them.

"I have. But after I talked to you, I realized that God gave me a different path. And I can sit and wish for things that didn't happen, or I could walk this path and do the very best that I can on it. Obviously the second choice is the best choice. And so, as much as I'm able, that's the choice I'm going to make."

She gave him a look, impressed that he had run that through in his mind and come up with that decision.

"Do you think you're going to regret that?" she finally asked.

He tilted his head. "I might. But I don't think anyone ever regrets doing what God wants them to do."

"And you think the candy shop is what God wants?"

He nodded, eyeing her, like her reaction mattered to him.

"I think that the only thing that you should do is what God wants you to do."

"That's kind of the conclusion I came to too. After all, the Bible does say that giving my life for God is reasonable service."

That wasn't an exact quote of that verse, but it was close, and she tucked that thought away. Most people dismissed that reasonable service that they were supposed to give to the Lord because of their gratefulness for salvation, but acted like God was like a genie in a bottle that was supposed to pop up when they needed Him, answer their prayers, give them everything they wanted, and then step back in the background and let them live their lives the way they wanted to. For a Christian, nothing could be further from the truth. But there were so many Christians she knew who lived their lives exactly like that, thinking God just wanted them to be happy.

He wanted them to choose happiness, of course, but it wasn't about living one's life for oneself. Ever. Not for a Christian. It was a lesson she was still learning.

"I think I could just stay here this evening and stare at these flowers. They're so pretty. Thank you," she said, giving Jack a shy glance. The flowers, the compliments, it was all very romantic. Was he seriously interested in her like that?

She hoped so, but she also didn't want to get her hopes up.

"Well then, let's go. I'm hungry." He allowed her to walk through the kitchen first and then opened the door for her.

Finally, she decided that she might as well just ask, so after she walked through the door, she stopped and turned around while he shut it.

"I've been trying to figure out whether this is an actual date, or just a celebration because you're grateful that I've been helping Lilly and you somehow think that I'm the reason that she was talking yesterday, or is it because you had things you wanted to tell me and you thought that going out to eat would give us some privacy?"

"Wow. That's a lot of choices. Could you run through those again?"

She blinked twice before she realized he was teasing her.

"This isn't funny!" she said, stomping her foot and putting her hands on her hips. She was only kind of half joking. He was teasing her, and she liked it, but she still wanted to know exactly what they were doing, so she could temper her expectations to match his intentions.

"I'm sorry. I shouldn't have joked about that. And you're right for asking. I could see how you would get confused."

"Okay. So it's not just me overthinking all of this."

"No, I suppose not." He had stopped in front of her, with the door shut, at the top of the steps. He shoved his hands in his pockets and looked out over the yard.

"I suppose I do have things I need to talk to you about, and it would be nice to have privacy, and it's true that I wanted to celebrate, because I do give you the credit for the fact that Lilly spoke yesterday. And I know," he held a hand out to keep her from saying anything, "you don't think it's all you, but I know that Lilly hadn't said anything for years before you got here, and you worked with her for a few weeks, and now she's talking. So you can take that however you want to, and so can I. And I'm giving you the credit."

She tilted her head, because it made sense when he said it like that.

"But I suppose that was just an excuse. Because I like you. I like you a lot. Not just because you helped my daughter, but because you're the kind of person who goes above and beyond what you need to. Obviously, you're caring and considerate and compassionate and funny, and willing to work hard, and I guess I could go on, but... I was afraid that you wouldn't be interested in me because of working with Lilly. And I definitely did not want you to be in trouble with the school in any way." He paused, but it seemed like he was going to say something else, so Kate kept her mouth closed.

"So yeah. I guess if I am laying my cards on the table, I asked you out on a date because I like you. I brought you the flowers because I like you. I might like you more than a little. It's possible that... I'm falling in love with you. And if that makes you uncomfortable, or if you're going to get in trouble for that, maybe we should figure that out now."

His eyes slid to hers, as he stood there, seeming to brace himself for whatever it was that she was going to say.

"Oh, Jack. I don't think the school will have any problem at all. If I were dating a client, that would be a professional issue, but the father of one of my students would certainly not be an issue, and I haven't even started working yet, so there shouldn't be any issues at all. As for me... I was afraid that you didn't feel for me the same way I felt for you. That's why I was worried that this was just you saying thank you, or you wanting to talk to me."

"So I think we figured out that we both like each other?" Jack said, uncertain, and Kate knew she was blushing. She felt like a teenager. "I think that's what we just figured out."

"Then I can hold your hand?" he asked, lifting a brow and pulling a hand out of his pocket and holding it palm up, waiting for her to slip her hand into his.

"Yeah. I guess that's what that means."

"Does that mean we're a couple?" he asked. "I guess I'm trying to figure out exactly what's going on, because... it's been a long time since I've done this, and you're a lot different than Lauren."

"I'd like to hear about Lauren," she said, ignoring the first part of his question. Probably she should think about it, but the words slipped out before she could stop them. "And yeah. I think we're a couple. Although... I don't date casually. I'm pretty serious about wanting to find that person that I want to settle down with, who wants to settle down with me and build a family together."

"I'm serious about that. I already have one child, and Lilly needs siblings. I've not been in a huge rush to find someone, just because Lilly has needed so much of my attention. But if she's going to continue to talk—"

"Did she speak more today?"

"A little. She's not jabbering around yet, but I do believe that she will be soon."

"That's great! I should have asked that immediately. I guess I was so wrapped up in being nervous about what you and I were doing together, and what this meant, that I totally didn't even think about it."

"I could have texted you and told you about it, but I guess I was thinking the same thing. What do you think of me? And what's going on with us?"

"I think we have that pretty much figured out, although I suppose I have a few things I should tell you too."

"Let's get in the car, at least make our way to the restaurant, and then we can talk about those things that we need to, okay?" He waited for her nod before he led the way down the steps and walked to his car, where he opened the door for her to get in.

Chapter Nineteen

*J*ack lifted his head to the cool December air and smiled. Kate truly did like him, and they were going to be a couple.

He walked around the car and opened her door, watching as she stood gracefully, and then holding his hand out and watching her slide her fingers into his.

Was there a better feeling in the world? He wasn't sure there was, and he felt like he was walking on air as he closed her door, and they walked toward the restaurant. Maybe the candy cane shop wouldn't make it. Maybe Lilly would never talk much. Maybe he would regret giving up the chance he had to farm with his brother. But it felt like all was right in the world, as long as Kate was beside him, and he knew he was doing what God wanted him to do.

They made it to the restaurant door, and he pulled it open, allowing Kate to walk forward, and then following as a host seated them.

They gave their drink orders and then perused the menus for a bit.

It was simple fare, nothing fancy, and he felt like he should be taking her to a much nicer place, but Kate didn't seem to care, and he really couldn't afford it.

"Maybe it's not fair of me to ask you to be with someone who has nothing. I mean, my shop is struggling, and I might not be successful after all."

"I don't care. If it doesn't make it, we'll figure something else out. Isn't that what success is? Just failing until you make it, right?"

He'd never heard that, but he had to laugh a little, then he lifted his shoulder. "I guess. You're sure that's not going to bother you?"

"No. It's not. Trying and failing is far better than not trying at all. And I'm completely behind you, no matter what."

"Then maybe you can help me figure out what I'm going to do for the festival. I wanted to make some kind of heritage candy that was really special, since I don't want to lose this opportunity to put my shop out there and snatch up all the great advertising that being the featured shop garners."

"Then I'll help you. I don't really know much about candy recipes, but I can search the Internet."

The waitress came, and they both gave their orders. He laughed as she ordered the special, which was what he had intended as well.

They shared a smile after the waitress left, and then he said, "Lauren had a bunch of recipes in the storage shed out back. Stuff that had been passed down from her parents and grandparents and great-grandparents. You might be able to find something in there. I just... I haven't taken the time to go through the things. But you're welcome to do whatever you'd like."

"All right. I can start there tomorrow after I get home from school."

"That would be perfect, unless you have something else you wanted to do?"

"My intention was to be with Lilly and help you. That fits right in with all of my plans." She smiled. "Plus, I really want you to do well with the festival."

"I need to talk to my brother about selling my share of the farm, but even if he agrees, I'm betting that he won't be able to come up with the money right away. I'm going to have to be able to make enough money from the festival to tide the store over until the money from the farm comes in. So, with my big supplier pulling out, a lot hinges on this."

"No pressure." She smiled, but he knew that she was taking it seriously, and he appreciated that.

Her hand sat in the middle of the table, now that she wasn't holding her menu, and he slid his over and put it on top of hers.

She turned her hand immediately, and their fingers threaded together.

There was just something about that that made him feel connected and at peace. He watched their fingers for a bit, noticing the differences and loving the fact that they were not the same.

"You had things you wanted to talk to me about?" she prompted him when he was quiet for a bit.

He looked at their hands for another few seconds before he raised his gaze to hers.

"I guess I just wanted to tell you a little bit about Lauren. I felt like you deserve to know, and especially now that you've agreed to be with me, and we're thinking about the future together. Not that there's a whole lot to tell."

"You don't have to if you don't want to."

"I don't necessarily want to, but I think you deserve it. After all, I was married before, and she's Lilly's mother, and you should know."

"Lilly obviously adored her."

"She did, and Lauren was a good mom. But she really was focused on the candy shop. And... I think our relationship suffered some, because she felt like she needed to call the shots all the time. I wanted us to stay together, especially after Lilly was on the way, and that's why I left the farm, moved into the candy shop, and went to be beside her. I suppose a lot of me resented that. Maybe that's what came between us, but by the time she died, we were barely talking. I... I don't want to allow my relationship to get like that in the future.

I should have told her how I felt, although in my defense, I did bring it up multiple times, and she told me that if I wanted to be a farmer, I could move back out to the farm and be a farmer, but she was going to stay right there. There was no discussion, and I felt like I made the only choice I could to keep our family together."

"Wow. I... I hope I don't do that. I hope I can be flexible enough that we can make a decision that benefits both of us."

"I guess that's where I was going with that. I feel like the candy shop is Lilly's heritage, but you and I have a life to live before Lilly grows up. I don't want to force you into being a candy cane maker's wife if that's not what you want."

"It doesn't matter to me. If you make candy canes, if you expand the shop, if you sell it and become a farmer, I don't care. I'm with you."

That made him feel right and good the whole way down to his soul, and he squeezed her hand.

Kate wasn't the kind of person who said things just to make him feel good, and he knew she meant exactly what she said.

"Even if I want to move to California?" he asked, only half joking.

"Where you go I will go," she said, and then continued, "your people will be my people and your God my God." She laughed a little.

"You can say that with ease. God's done too much for me for me to ever turn my back on Him now."

"It's good to hear. It's nice to see gratefulness too. I think so many times we just expect that God owes us, and we forget that it's the other way around—we all owe a debt we cannot pay, couldn't even hope to begin to repay."

"Yeah. It's an unfathomable debt."

The waitress brought their food, and he waited until she left before he continued. "But we're to serve Him out of love, not because we have to."

"True. But following Jesus is one little decision after another, to not fulfill the lusts of the flesh, but to follow after the spirit. Each decision builds on the next, until you have a lifetime."

"That's the truth. Sometimes we lose sight of the big picture."

His food looked delicious, and they prayed and then began to eat.

"What did you want to talk about?" he asked.

Kate had her mouth full, and she finished chewing and swallowed before she spoke.

"Last year this time I was engaged to be married."

He blinked, feeling like he'd gotten punched in the gut.

"Engaged?"

"We were serious. I'm sorry, I guess this is something you should have known before, but I didn't know that you and I were headed in this direction."

"No. I'm surprised, but it's fine. I understand why that probably wasn't the thing that you would introduce yourself with: 'Hi, I'm Kate, I was engaged last year.'"

She laughed, as he had intended, and it made him feel better too. So she'd been engaged. Wow.

"He broke up with me on Christmas morning. I thought I would never trust anyone again. You know, the way it always happens— after someone betrays you in that big of a way, you think you're never going to do it again. But you are so much different than he was. I couldn't imagine him loving his daughter the way you love Lilly, and being faithful to anything the way you've been faithful to the candy shop. You're just completely different, and it isn't really even that much of a stretch for me to know that you'll stay with me forever."

That made him feel good. For sure. Those were words that a man could use to keep himself warm for a very long time.

"So that's one of the things you like about me?" he asked softly.

"Your faithfulness? Your dedication? Your perseverance, and your love for your daughter? All of those things are things I love about you. They make you the kind of man that a woman can admire and depend on."

He didn't realize that their meal was going to be a series of her making him feel like he was ten feet tall and could do anything. It was a shock to know that she'd been engaged, but to be compared so favorably to her broken engagement definitely eased that in his mind.

"I don't want to be presumptuous, but I guess I don't want to draw things out too long. I want to make sure that Lilly is okay with us, and that you're sure—"

"I'm sure. And I don't think we need to worry too much about Lilly. Especially since she began to talk whenever you came. It's obvious that she's okay with her mom being in heaven, and she wants a new mother. I... I couldn't help but think when she was saying that that I wanted her new mother to be you."

Kate's cheeks turned a becoming shade of pink.

He figured, while he was embarrassing her, he could go on. "I would like to have more children too. I'm hoping that might be something you're interested in?"

She nodded. "I love kids. That's part of the reason I became what I did, so I could be around them all day long. But I've always wanted a family of my own."

"It's okay that it's a little bit ready-made?"

"That makes it even better. Lilly is an angel, and I adore her almost as much as I adore her father."

Maybe it was the company, but Jack figured he'd never eaten such great food, and they shared a banana split for dessert. Then they walked hand-in-hand along the river, despite the cold. His heart felt warm and happy.

Kate seemed to be in the same kind of frame of mind. Neither one of them wanted to go home.

But they both had to get up early, and so reluctantly, he led her back to the car, opening the door for her, and drove her to the farmhouse.

"I forgot to leave my light on. Thankfully, the walkway is pretty flat."

"There is that one crack in it that's been there since I was a kid. I'll walk you in."

She gave him a grateful smile, and he wasn't sure whether it was because he was walking her in, whether she was actually scared of tripping on the crack, or she just didn't want the evening to end either.

Regardless, she waited for him to come around and open her door, and then they walked hand in hand up the path that he had walked all his life.

"You grew up here?" she asked softly.

"I did. Up until I was in junior high, and then my parents built the bigger farmhouse that Bryan lives in now."

"And he's not married?" she asked.

"No."

"Which direction is it?" she asked as they reached the end of the walk and climbed the stairs to the door.

"It's about a half a mile that direction. Just keep following the driveway, and you come to the barn first, then you go past that, and the house is beyond it."

"What were you guys going to do with this house?"

"I guess he was thinking about renting it out. I really didn't have any thoughts about it at all. That's part of the reason I didn't offer it to you to begin with. It just wasn't on my radar. I've been so focused on the candy shop."

They had stopped and turned to face each other. He lifted a hand to her cheek. "Right now, I was thinking about kissing you good night."

"I like that thought," she said easily, and she turned her face up to his.

Moonlight shone down, and a few stray snowflakes floated past.

"I think this will go down as one of the best nights of my life. Definitely one of the best weeks. Lilly started talking after years, and I am with the most amazing woman I've ever met in my entire life. I really don't see how life could get better." He shivered. "It's a little scary. If it can't get better, there's only one way for it to go."

"And whatever happens, we'll handle it. It doesn't matter which direction it goes."

He loved that—that she was so secure in what God wanted for her life, knowing that He wanted the best for her, that whatever happened, she'd see the best in it and be content. That was inspiring.

"I love that about you."

"I love you."

He grinned. "I love you too."

He lowered his head and kissed her gently, pleased when her arms came around his neck and pulled him closer.

He didn't kiss her long—it was really cold—not nearly as long as he wanted to.

"I really don't want tonight to end," he whispered softly as he lifted his head.

"Same." Her eyes sparkled up into his.

"I like the idea of a short courtship." He was only half joking.

She smiled, but she nodded. "I really like that idea too."

"We'll have to talk about that sometime soon." He sighed. "In the meantime, I better get home. Mrs. Abernathy is probably asleep on my couch."

"Oh. I don't envy you the job of waking her up and getting her home."

"She said that I can let her stay there. I might tonight. I think I would like to keep the good memories close."

"Text me when you get home?" she said.

He nodded. And then, even though he knew he shouldn't, he lowered his head and kissed her once more. It was a beautiful night, perfect in every way.

Chapter Twenty

Kate hummed softly as she and Lilly knelt down in the storage shed, elbows deep in one of the boxes that she'd opened.

Lilly had started chattering, like a normal child her age, and Kate listened, nodding and smiling and commenting when she needed to.

Lilly went on about her day, her friends, what she'd done with Mrs. Abernathy the night before, and how she used to play in the storage shed when her mother was still alive.

Whoever had said that once the dam broke, the words would come gushing out, had been absolutely right.

Kate was curious as to whether Lilly would ever tell them why she had chosen not to speak for three entire years, but she supposed it didn't really matter. From a clinical and professional standpoint, she would really love to know the reasoning, because perhaps if she could understand why, she could figure out how to break another child's silence. Although she knew no two children were alike, still, as a professional, she was curious. As Lilly's potential mother, she just loved the little girl.

"Look, that's Mommy's old cookbook," Lilly said, interrupting her monologue about the frog they'd seen at recess.

"This?" Kate asked in disbelief. It didn't look like a cookbook. It looked more like a photo album. She'd been avoiding picking it up because as much as she was interested in seeing Jack when he was younger, she wasn't sure she wanted to see him embracing another woman. She knew that was a part of his life before, and she accepted that, but perhaps she just didn't want to rub her face in it.

Any more than Jack would want to see pictures of her snuggled up to her ex-fiancé, whom she hadn't thought about in a long time, interestingly. When she'd come, part of the reason she'd taken the job was to get away from everything, and she'd thought that it would be a long time before she got over him.

It was funny that she took one look at Jack and her ex-fiancé had vanished from her head.

"Mommy had some really good recipes in there. She said someday we would make them all. She said there were some that she hadn't made in years, and others that she had never made."

"Some she had never made?" Kate asked with interest as she pulled what looked like a photo album out of the box.

"She said great-great-grandma used to make some of them, and someday we would make candy canes like great-grandma."

Kate was a little confused about how many great-grandmas there were, but it didn't really matter, because she understood the implications—the recipes in this book hadn't been seen for generations, and they were perfect for what Jack wanted for the festival. It would bring attention and, hopefully, sales.

"I think your mama was saving this book for a special occasion, and I'm pretty sure the festival is the exact special occasion she had in mind," Kate said as they carefully opened the book and turned the pages of the handwritten recipes that were placed in the photo album and protected by the plastic page protectors.

"Are they good recipes?" Lilly asked, looking at the recipes and then glancing up at Kate's face.

"I think we'll let your dad be the judge of that. I'm pretty sure he's going to be excited to see this. Shall we take it in to him?"

"Yeah. You carry it. It's too heavy for me."

It was a big book, but Kate was excited and barely noticed as she climbed up, dusted herself off, and held Lilly's hand as they walked into the back of the shop.

"Daddy! Daddy! I think we found something that you're going to want to see!"

"Oh really?" Jack asked, coming to the doorway where the back room met the shop, with a towel in his hands, drying them off. "What's that?"

"This!" Lilly said, theatrically pointing to the book Kate held.

"I don't know if these are what you are hoping for or not, but I wanted you to take a look at them."

Immediately interest lit Jack's eyes, although there was still a glow in them—maybe from last night, or maybe it was just the way he was going to look at her from now on—but it made her feel like he loved her and was happy to be with her.

"Let's see what you've got." He walked a little closer, throwing the towel over his shoulder, his eyes on the book. "I don't think I've ever seen that before." He took it from Kate's hands. "Where'd you guys get it? In the storage shed?"

"Yeah," Lilly said.

"It was in the back, in a blue tub."

"A blue tub?" Jack scrunched up his nose, thinking. "When her mother moved, she gave us a bunch of stuff of her great-grandmother's and said that it was antiques and the like. Lauren said she'd get to it eventually and stuck it in the back. Anything that didn't have anything to do with the candy shop, she wasn't interested in."

"I could see how she might have missed it. I didn't think it was anything special either. It looked like a photo album. But Lilly said that her mom said that it had some good recipes in it."

"That's what she told me in my dream."

Kate and Jack exchanged a look.

"Which dream was that, honey?" Jack said, sounding curious but not concerned.

"The one I had when I fell asleep at her funeral. She said I wasn't supposed to tell anyone until it was time."

"You weren't supposed to tell anyone until it was time for what?" Jack asked, his hands still, his eyes on his daughter.

"I don't know. She just said until it was time. And I didn't know when it was going to be time, so I knew I couldn't say anything."

Now it made sense. Jack lifted his eyes, and he shared a look with Kate that stretched between them, understanding dawning on both of their faces. That was why Lilly hadn't felt like she was able to talk—because she had a secret to keep, until it was time.

"Well, I think you did a good job. It's definitely time for us to know about this. Thank you for waiting like your mother asked and for letting me know now." He paused. "Next time, maybe you can let us know while you're still talking."

"I forgot how much I like to talk. I don't think I'm ever going to not talk again," Lilly said, which made Kate laugh.

"Please don't ever stop," Kate said.

"I agree. We love to hear you talk." Jack glanced at Kate, and they nodded together. Then he continued to open the book.

Kate held her breath while Jack perused the recipes.

It didn't take long to see the glowing excitement on his face and know that they had stumbled into something really good.

"Thank you, guys. This is exactly what we need."

Chapter Twenty-One

"I'm so glad the storm they forecast turned out to be nothing," Marjorie McBride said as she and Kate walked down the main street, banners bookmarking either end, announcing the huge Mistletoe Meadows All Day Christmas Festival.

"Same. I would have felt so bad for everyone who put all of the work into it, only to have people not show up because of snow. Would we have rescheduled?"

Marjorie sighed as they continued to walk slowly. Kate was careful not to go too fast. Marjorie was back on her feet, and said there was nothing wrong, but she still seemed very tired.

"We've never had it happen before. But I guess we would—for next Saturday. Although I don't think rescheduled things ever do as well as they do if they happen on the date they originally intended them to."

"I agree. Anyway, I guess we don't have to worry about that this year. It's a beautiful day."

"And it's warm too," Marjorie said with a smile.

Kate nodded, and they chatted some about the different things that were happening and the things that they were overseeing. Both of them had agreed that they were not going to be in charge of anything themselves, but delegated everything they could, just in case something came up and someone wasn't able to do what they had volunteered for. As far as Kate knew, everyone was manning their booths and doing their jobs.

"How is Terry doing?" Kate asked as they finished their walk down the street, noting that everything was going well.

Kate's eyes caught on Ben, the sheriff, as he talked with his preteen son. Rumor had it that Ben had moved back in with his mother because of a nasty divorce and the fact that his son had started acting out. Whatever the reason, he'd been a true blessing to Mistletoe Meadows since his return.

Kate felt bad for the boy and for Ben. She had seen Trent at school, and he seemed angry and belligerent. She didn't know if there was anything she could do for him or not, but she was going to be trying.

"She's doing okay. It's so hard to juggle everything that she's doing—a new baby, another one on the way, and a practice that's bursting at the seams. Hopefully the doctor that she has been speaking with who is going to come as a partner in her practice will be showing up soon. It certainly couldn't happen soon enough for her."

"They do seem to have a lot going on."

"But I don't think they could be happier. They just love their lives, and I'm so happy for them."

Indeed, Marjorie glowed when she talked about her children and the good choices that they had made. She knew that seeing one's children grow up and live for the Lord made a parent's heart happy.

Marjorie sighed. "I wish Isadora could get things straightened out. It just seems like she lost her zest for life when her marriage crumbled. It's been several years, and she's just not been able to get it back together."

"I don't blame her. You think that you've got your life all planned out and that things are going to go well, and then the person that you trusted betrays you in a way that it's so hard to get over."

"Sounds like you're talking from experience, but it seems like you and Jack are doing pretty well together."

"This time last year I was engaged to be married, and my fiancé broke up with me on Christmas morning. But you're right about Jack. I didn't think I'd ever forget about my fiancé or get over his betrayal, but Jack just erased all of that from my mind, and the future looks happy and exciting once more."

"I'm praying that happens for Isadora. She needs it."

"I'll pray for her too. I wish everyone could be as happy as I am right now."

"I just saw Ben go into the candy shop, but maybe you can go ahead on over and spend the rest of the day with Jack. Seems like he's doing a pretty good business and could use a hand. Everything else seems to be under control."

"Well, thank you, I think I will. It looked like Olivia and Noah are doing just as well as Jack, and I'm happy for them."

There were other stores up and down the street as well, although the new restaurant hadn't been able to open in time. There was some red tape that they just couldn't quite get through. Kate wasn't sure whether the restaurant would be open by Christmas or not. Seemed like that would be the date to aim for in a town like Mistletoe Meadows.

"We can check in together in a bit," Kate said.

"I'll text you if I need anything." Marjorie gave her a shooing motion with her hand, and Kate waved and grinned.

Marjorie was the best. She enjoyed helping with the festival, but her heart was most definitely with Jack and Lilly. And indeed, they did need help as she stepped into the store.

It was so packed, Ben hadn't even made it over to talk to Jack.

"It's good to see you out today, Ben. I hope you do nothing but enjoy yourself and have no official business to take care of."

It would be sad to have some kind of business the sheriff needed to take care of during their festival.

"I just hope my presence is deterrent enough. But it's my job, so I'm going to do what I can to make sure things go smoothly."

"It's good to see you. Reassuring."

"Tell Jack I said hi. Looks to me like he's too busy to chat, which I'm happy about, for sure."

"If you want something, I'm sure he'll make time for you."

"I was going to buy a few things—I've got some Christmas shopping to take care of—but I'll come back later." He glanced around the store. "Although you guys might be sold out by the looks of things."

"Yeah. It's been so much better than I hoped it was going to be."

"You and Marjorie deserve a lot of the credit. You spent a lot of hours planning, and then the execution took even more time."

"The McBride family helps a lot, and so did Jack, and I saw you out hanging banners last weekend, so I think the whole town deserves the credit."

"Nothing like a small town to pull together."

There was wisdom in Ben's eyes that seemed like it might have been hard-earned, and Kate thought again about Marjorie saying he'd come back after a nasty divorce, bringing his son with him.

Kate had heard about a few things the secret saint had done, not just for Ben but other needy families around town, and she thought again about how much she loved being in a small town where people cared about each other and did everything they could to help. So much different than where she had been before.

She missed it in a way, but in another way, she saw the breakup with her fiancé and the need to move out of Baltimore as things that had propelled her into the best time of her life. At the time, she wouldn't have thought they ever could have been worked out for good, but they absolutely had.

She thought again about being content with where God placed her and choosing to be happy and look at the positive. Right there was proof that things could work out if she didn't dwell on how terrible everything was. She could have holed up in her apartment, clung to a terrible job, and insisted that God needed to change things so they went her way.

And then she'd still be miserable and unhappy.

Instead, she'd almost by accident chosen the best way—to move on and to look for something better. And she'd found it.

Jack smiled as he saw her, and she walked over beside him, helping to pack up the candy canes that the customer in front of him had just bought.

They spent hours that day side by side, working together, with Lilly giving out free samples that they had made and packaged just for that very reason.

Lilly glowed and spoke with customers with an ease that hid the fact that she hadn't spoken at all for three years.

By the time the day was over, they were all exhausted, but very, very happy.

There were still several hours left, but the big crowds had gone, when Jack found a few minutes to take her aside.

"I was able to speak with my brother yesterday, but I didn't get a chance to tell you about it."

"What did he say?" Kate asked eagerly. On one hand, she wasn't sure that Jack really wanted to give up his farming dream, but on the other, she was really hoping that his brother would be able to buy him out, and Jack would be able to move forward with the plans and dreams he had for the candy shop. He really seemed to be getting invested in them, and maybe he'd needed to get over his resentment of his late wife before he could invest himself in the future of the candy shop and let the farm go.

"He said that he would talk to his bank, but he thought it would be a go. It would just take him a little while to come up with a down payment. He said he had some cattle that he could sell, and that should give him enough so the bank would loan him the rest. He said three or four months, tops."

"So he's interested in buying the whole farm, and he just needs a little bit of time to come up with the money. Jack, that's great!"

"I thought so too. I... I know this is kind of crazy, but I wanted to know if you would be interested in marrying me once all of that goes through?"

"Is this a proposal?" she asked, a little uncertain.

"I guess so. A spur-of-the-moment proposal where I don't even have a ring. But I was just so excited that it was all falling into place that it felt like the perfect time to say something. We both agreed we didn't want to mess around."

"Yeah." Kate felt excitement and fear and anticipation swirl inside of her, but one thing that she didn't have was uncertainty. "Yes. If this is a proposal, I'm saying yes. If this is a precursor, I will say yes when the time comes."

"All right. I don't know what it was, but yes was all I wanted to hear."

Jack grinned as he stroked her cheek with his fingertips and then lightly touched his lips to hers. "I wanted to do that all day."

"I've waited for you to do that all day," Kate murmured.

He took that opportunity then to kiss her properly, before the bell above the door rang, and they broke apart, reluctantly, knowing there were still customers to be served.

"I said the day we had our date that I didn't know if I could be happier, but I'm definitely happier now," Jack whispered to her.

"It does feel like a beautiful new beginning, doesn't it?"

"Yeah. I know there are going to be hard times, but I wish I could bottle this feeling up and pull it out when we need it, because it's the best feeling in the world."

"I love you, Jack," Kate said.

"I love you too. Merry Christmas."

❄

Join Jessie's list and be the first to know about new releases and sales on her books!

Read *Mistletoe Dreams*, the next book in the Mistletoe Meadows series, where a disgraced doctor and a guarded sheriff are thrown together by a town festival—and a troubled teen who just might need them both. Can healing hearts lead to unexpected love? Keep reading for a sneak peek now.

Sneak Peek of Mistletoe Dreams

"I'm really hoping we can open the clinic on Saturdays now that you're here," Dr. Terry Landis said to Dr. Hannah Reynolds.

Hannah nodded her head. "Although, I understand that you also need to slow down some," she said, eyeing Terry's stomach with a lifted brow.

Terry gave a guilty smile. "I know I need to. My husband, Judd, has been awesome about helping with the children, but this is our third child in three years, and I really don't want to miss these years with them."

"Nor should you have to. That's what I'm here for." Hannah put a hand on Terry's shoulder, and Terry smiled gratefully. There was a tightness around her eyes and dark circles beneath them that bespoke the extra hours and long nights she had pulled trying to keep her clinic solvent and trying to keep her family happy. Also, the pregnancy had taken a toll on her as well.

Hannah was thankful that she had been able to take the job, since Terry seemed like a really sweet person and would be easy and fun to work with.

Unlike her last, exceptionally high-pressure job.

A sour feeling started in her stomach, and she tried to pivot away from going back down memory lane. Although it was not easy. When someone made a monstrous mistake and was threatened with a multimillion-dollar lawsuit, a person had a tendency to not forget.

Not that Hannah wanted to forget necessarily. She did not. A person could always learn from their mistakes.

But those had been some of the darkest days of her life, and not just because of her own problems. She hadn't wanted to make a mistake on anyone's medical care. No matter how honest, sincere, and well-intentioned the mistake was.

"For now though, take the weekend to settle into your new place. I don't think you told me where you were staying." Terry clicked off on the ipad she had been sharing with Hannah and pushed back away from the desk, so that they could make eye contact as the computer powered down.

"Several years ago when my grandmother passed away, I inherited her house." She paused for a moment, thinking about all of the memories that were entangled with the house and her grandmother and Mistletoe Meadows. She'd spent many happy summers here. And in fact, she and Terry had played as children. But that had been a long time ago. "It's in desperate need of some cleaning and some repairs as well. I was here over the summer taking a look at it when I applied for the job. It's livable, but it needs work."

"If you need any help, let me know."

"I will. It's nice to know that I have people in town I can depend on, but I'm probably not going to bother you unless I really need to. You look exhausted."

"I could go for some sleep," Terry admitted. "But I think once you get settled into your new position and the townspeople get used to you, I'll be able to take a bit more time off."

"Hopefully before the baby comes." Hannah lifted a brow but didn't probe further.

"She's due right around Christmas," Terry said, as though she could read Hannah's mind.

Hannah had wondered but didn't want to ask.

"Once we get settled in, we'll have to talk about my maternity leave. I have several thoughts in mind, but I definitely want it to be something that works for you as well."

"Fair enough. I don't think I'll have any trouble getting my bearings. Everything looks fairly straightforward, and you have things very well organized."

"And the people are awesome. Not just with visiting the clinic, but with helping out too. It's not just me that would help you if you needed it unpacking. Most people are excited about the new doctor in town."

"I'm excited to be back in Mistletoe Meadows. I loved spending time here when I was a kid visiting my grandmother. I never dreamed I would actually live here one day."

That was an understatement. She'd always thought she would go to the big city and have a prestigious practice as a doctor in a large, possibly teaching hospital. She hadn't really understood all the ins and outs of the medical education that she would have when she was younger, but she certainly hadn't pictured coming back and working in a small clinic in a tiny town.

Right now, though, that sounded like just what she needed to get her life and career back on track.

"All right. I'll meet you back here Monday morning, and we'll have you shadow me for the first few days to see how things go. Then, when you're feeling pretty confident, we'll discuss scheduling."

"Fair enough," Hannah said, as Terry pushed her bulky body to a standing position and waddled to the door, which she opened for Hannah.

"There are plenty of things to get involved with, if you're interested," she said by way of conversation as they started walking out of the clinic.

"I definitely would like to get involved in the town," Hannah said. But she also knew she had a tendency to bite off more than she could chew at times. Although she really thought the best thing she could do was to stay busy. Was she going to stay here for a long time?

It was a question she didn't have an answer for. But just because she wasn't quite sure how long she'd be in town didn't mean that she wasn't going to help wherever she could.

"There's a town meeting for organizing the Christmas festival. We're actually more on the ball this year, and we're beginning to organize in November rather than waiting until the last minute the way we usually do."

"From what I hear, whether you organize last minute or not, the festival is a hit throughout the state."

"That's part of the reason we're beginning to organize earlier. We're expecting a record turnout this year. We've had some unexpected publicity and a lot of interest, despite the fact the calendar says it's still early."

"Well, good for you then. It's always good to be prepared."

"I agree. Anyway, you're welcome to attend, and if you feel better going with someone, you're welcome to come with me."

"I appreciate that. I might feel a little bit weird walking in by myself, so it'd be nice to walk in with someone who knows what they're doing."

"I wouldn't go that far. It might be more like the blind leading the blind, but it's always nice to have someone beside you when you don't know what you're doing."

"I couldn't agree more."

They talked about the date and the time and made arrangements for Hannah to go to Dr. Terry's house to meet, and then they'd arrive at the meeting together.

Hannah left feeling like not only did she get a good job, but she made a friend. Terry McBride seemed like a very down-to-earth, friendly, and sweet woman. And if the busyness of the clinic was any indication, the townspeople loved her.

Hopefully, Hannah could learn from her and be just as beloved by the town.

Sign up for Jessie's newsletter! Get a free book, access to exclusive bonus content, get fun and funny updates on her life on the farm and more!

A Gift from Jessie

View this code through your smart phone camera to be taken to a page where you can download a FREE ebook when you sign up to get updates from Jessie Gussman! Find out why people say, "Jessie's is the only newsletter I open and read" and "You make my day brighter. Love, love, love reading your newsletters. I don't know where you find time to write books. You are so busy living life. A true blessing." and "I know from now on that I can't be drinking my morning coffee while reading your newsletter – I laughed so hard I sprayed it out all over the table!"

Claim your free book from Jessie!